THE POWER OF THREE

THE POWER OF THREE

THE TRIAD SERIES, BOOK 1

KATE PEARCE

PROLOGUE

PLANET PAVLOVAN, TRIOS SYSTEM, 229982

"*Second* Male? No. That can't be right."

The Oracle stared right through Esca. Her beautiful face disinterested, immune both to his shock, and to his highly inappropriate question. She was too deep in her trance with the deities of their planet to care what he thought.

"*Esca!*" He turned to see his father gesticulating wildly. "Thank the Oracle, and withdraw!"

He bowed his head, but he couldn't force himself to say thank you. He stumbled down the marble steps toward his parents, who hustled him away from the main hall of the temple and into one of the side rooms. His mother was already weeping, his father as pale as the stonework.

"How can I be Second Male? I graduated first in my class from military school! Everyone knows I have a brilliant career ahead of me! How in frek's name am I supposed to bow down to another male?"

His father took a deep breath. "The Oracle has spoken. We cannot go against the decision of the gods." He looked past Esca to the priestess who had come into the room behind him. "My lady, do you have news of the male my son is to join with?"

1

Esca turned his back on his father and glared at the priestess. His graduation day was in ruins He'd always known he'd be in a relationship with two others; it was the way of his people. But he'd assumed he'd be First Male, preferably to two females, certainly not the inferior position of *Second* to another man.

The woman bowed, handed Esca a scroll, and departed. He slowly unrolled the parchment and read the single word.

"Ash. Who the *frek* is that?"

"*Ash?*" His father's jaw literally dropped. "He's the newest member of the Senate. By the gods, if you are allied to him you will be *untouchable*."

"Not by him," Esca snapped. "Who is this man? If he's on the council, he's probably ancient."

"He's only about seven or eight years older than you are." His father's expression was lightening with every second. "He is *extraordinary*." He turned to his wife. "If Esca is allied to him, Marnee, we can be proud."

"And what about me?" Esca demanded. "I'm the one who has to live with the guy, has to let him—"

"Let's go home and discuss this further." His father wasn't even listening to him anymore.

Esca turned on his heel and started down the stairs. In the entrance hall of the temple, a uniformed man looked up and stepped forward.

"Are you Esca?"

"Yes."

The man bowed. "Ash would like to meet you. I am here to take you to him." He smiled at Esca's parents. "I shall return him to you before dusk."

Esca didn't bother to talk to the man on the way through the city. What the *frek* was he supposed to say to this Ash guy? The last thing his father had said before he'd been escorted to the limo, was not to disgrace his family. How was he going to do that when he'd been put in an impossible situation?

They arrived at one of the premier apartment buildings in the city, and Esca was taken in a private elevator that went up so fast he almost puked. The elevator opened onto a narrow white marble vestibule. His companion knocked on the only door, and led Esca through into a large room that was almost all windows and offered a stunning view over the capital city.

"One moment, sir. I'll go and find Senator Ash."

His driver disappeared. Esca focused his gaze on the distant lights of the military base where he'd hoped to begin his career. His throat hurt and his gut was tied in knots. But he had to do the right thing, the reputation of his family depended on it.

A slight sound behind him made him turn. His gaze took in the long fair hair and perfect features of the man who studied him with equal interest. And *frek*, not only was his face good to look at, but his mind… the psychic power emanating from him called to something deep inside Esca, made him want to move closer…

"Esca? I'm Ash."

Swallowing hard, Esca moved forward and fell to his knees in front of the other man. He formally kissed Ash's fingers.

"First Male."

"Thank you for observing the traditions. I appreciate it." Ash withdrew his hand. "Now will you come and sit down? Let me offer you a drink. We have a lot to discuss."

Esca rose to his feet aware that although he was as tall as Ash, he was already broader, and going to get even bigger.

"But aren't you going to—"

"Take you straight to bed and ravish you?" Ash's smile was sweet. "That isn't really my style."

Esca subsided into the nearest chair and waited until Ash gave him a drink and took the seat opposite him. "You don't want me?"

"You've just graduated from military school, and you're due to attend the space academy, correct?"

"That's what I wanted to do, yes."

"Then I suggest you go ahead and do it." He looked up and Esca noticed how blue his eyes were. "The only difference will be that instead of going to your parents when you're on leave, I'd like you to come here. I'd like you to start thinking of this as your home."

"I don't understand." Esca tried not to scowl. "You could make me live here permanently, and stop me from being anything, but your mate."

Ash raised his eyebrows. "Why would I do that? Don't you think you deserve to fulfill your dreams?"

Esca let out his breath. "I want to be the best space fighter pilot our military has ever produced."

"Then do it." Ash toasted him with his glass. "We have all our lives to get to know each other."

"I never imagined I'd have to—to—"

"Submit to another male?"

"Yeah." Esca raised his chin. "I always thought I'd be First Male."

"I can see why. From what I've read, you have extraordinary potential both in the military and as a psychic match for me." He hesitated. "Do you feel that, at least?"

"That I'm drawn to what's going on in your head?" Esca nodded. "Yeah, I get that loud and clear. It's the other stuff I'm not so sure about." He looked hastily down at his empty glass. "I've never been in a physical relationship with a male."

"I know, which is why I'm not pushing that on you right now."

"Right now?"

Ash smiled. "One day, I hope you'll come willingly to my bed." He shrugged. "I can wait."

1

PLANET PAVLOVAN, 229990

8 years later

"Congratulations, on your new command, Major."

Esca smiled at the assembled guests, and raised his glass to accept the toast.

"Thanks. I always wanted to be a fighter pilot, but apparently the military had other plans for me." He grinned at his assembled team. "I'm more than happy to lead this new Special Forces unit."

"Good luck with that with this war going on." Grumbled his cousin, Trenx. "As captain of the ship, you're going to be based on, I'll do my best to keep you all alive."

"Thanks. We appreciate it." Esca turned to Ash who had come up behind him and was refilling his glass. "We've got an early start tomorrow, so don't give me too much."

Trenx groaned. "That's right. We've got to be going anyway." He raised his voice. "All of you except Senator Ash, and Major Esca, we're returning to base."

"You don't want me to come?" Esca asked.

"Nope, you get the night off to celebrate." Trenx winked at him. "But be on board in eight hours, or we'll go without you."

By the time his shipmates and assorted guests had been waved off, the caterers were done cleaning up, and Ash had disappeared. Esca thanked Chase, their housekeeper, and went through to his suite to finally strip off his dress uniform. Even though he scrubbed his dark hair twice and spent a long time in the shower, he emerged wide-awake, and aware that Ash hadn't gone to bed either.

He sat down on the side of his bed and clasped his hands together. Since his last leave, he'd been dreaming constantly about the other man, waking up hard and wanting, imagining their limbs entangled, Ash moving over him...

He was twenty-five. Old enough now to understand the power the other male had over him, and want to put it to the test.

"*Frek.*"

He'd never turned his back on a challenge but this was damned hard. With a sigh, he got up, wrapped a towel around his hips and headed back across the now deserted main living area to Ash's bedroom suite. He knocked on the door and waited until he heard Ash's reply before going in.

His First Male sat in a chair by the fire. From the look of his long damp blond hair he'd also showered. He wore a white silk robe, knotted at his waist and his feet were bare. He looked up as Esca entered.

"Is something wrong?"

Esca gathered his courage and went to kneel at Ash's feet. "I have a confession to make."

"You don't want this assignment? I can—"

Esca wrapped his fingers around Ash's ankle. "If you use your influence to protect me, I'll bloody kill you. It's not about that."

"Then what?"

"I can't stop thinking about you." Esca managed to look up. "I kept wondering which of our guests you were dating, or, or fucking, or—"

Ash touched his hair. "I haven't fucked anyone since we were formally mated."

"That's almost eight years ago!"

He shrugged. "I was convinced you would be worth the wait."

Esca groaned. "*Frek*, I wish I could say the same, I've fucked way too many females, I didn't know you'd *wait*."

"No males?"

"No, you're the only one I've ever—" He swallowed hard. "Ever wanted that way."

"Well, that's good isn't it?"

Esca kissed Ash's elegant foot. "So will you fuck me?"

"If that is what you wish."

"Tonight?"

"Why this sudden rush?"

"Because I keep thinking about all the time I've wasted because of my own stupid pride, all the psychic power I've denied you by refusing to complete our bond."

"I've done fairly well without you." There was a hint of amusement in Ash's voice that made Esca relax. "But additional psychic power is always appealing to a man of my political appetites."

"Then will you take mine?"

"With pleasure." Ash stood and headed for his bedroom. "Come, then."

ASH LED Esca into his bedroom and closed the door. At first sight, the Oracle couldn't have chosen a more unlikely mate for him than this hardened soldier who still looked rather unsure of what he'd let himself in for. Esca wasn't a man used to submitting to anyone, his sheer strength of will and physique shouted that. Even at eighteen, his arrogance and courage had impressed Ash. At twenty-six he was breathtaking. Ash considered the flex of his Second's muscles, the tight abs and long legs. He'd waited a long time to lure his mate into his bed, and he was determined not to frek it up now.

"Sit." Ash pointed at the side of the bed and Esca did what he asked. He sat like the military man he was, feet spread wide, shoulders back and his hands on his knees.

Ash approached and put his hands on the other man's shoulders, felt his own shock at the intimate contact echoed in Esca's mind. Gods, he wanted this man. Reaching out with all his senses, he slid his hands down over Esca's arms and muscled chest, letting him access his mind in a way he allowed no other, letting him feel what he was feeling.

He stroked over Esca's nipples until they were hard against his palm and then used his finger and thumb to make them even harder.

"Ah..."

Ash smiled as he noted Esca's cock filling out and pushing against the confines of his towel. He kissed Esca's nose and then his forehead.

"What did you imagine it would be like, Second Male?"

"Like this," Esca whispered against Ash's lips. "Like I wouldn't want to stop, that I'd end up begging you to do anything you wanted to me."

Ash's own cock thickened at that admission, and he bit gently at Esca's lip. "Are you hard for me?"

"Yes."

Ash dropped his hand lower until he grasped Esca's hard cock through his towel. "May I see you?"

"*Yes.*"

Ash pulled the towel away and fell to his knees. "Beautiful." He leaned forward and licked Esca's already wet cock from tip to root.

"Aren't I supposed to be doing that to you?"

Ash smiled up at him. "Eventually—unless you object to me touching you first."

"Gods, no, go ahead, I'm—"

Ash swallowed Esca's cock in one smooth motion, easing him down his throat and sucking hard. He wanted to smile at his mate's reaction, the way his hips thrust forward to push himself deeper and his hand buried in Ash's hair holding him in a tight painful grip. He took his time getting to know what Esca liked, keeping him aroused and hard, only easing off when he sensed it was too much. Being able to access his partner's chaotic thoughts made the process so much easier and much more intimate. While he sucked, he brought his hand up to play with Esca's balls and explore the soft skin of his taint and the pucker of his ass.

"Oh *frek*, I'm—"

Ash swallowed Esca's come and then carefully released his lover's now flaccid cock. He stood and gestured for Esca to lie back on the bed. He climbed up beside him and slowly took off his robe. Esca's gaze lowered.

"You're big."

"Don't worry, I'll fit." Ash straddled Esca's stomach and cupped his cock and balls. "Give me your hand."

Esca complied and Ash wrapped it around both of their cocks, intertwining his fingers with his lover's. Wetness soon covered their moving fingers. Ash carefully leaned forward and brushed his mouth over Esca's parted lips.

"Do you like this?"

"Yes."

"Do you want to come again, or will you wait?"

"I'll do whatever you want as long as you don't stop touching me."

"Oh, I'm not stopping now. Not until I'm so deep inside you that there's nowhere else to go." Ash smiled as he picked up the lube he'd placed by the side of the bed and coated his finger.

He disentangled himself, leaving the other man holding his own shaft and knelt between his legs. As he licked the crown of Esca's cock he eased the tip of his finger inside him, felt a tremor run through his mate and distracted him with more licks and kisses.

It was no hardship to take his time. He'd dreamed of this moment for years, Esca willingly spread beneath him, begging to be fucked. The reality was even better than he'd expected. He pushed in further, to the first knuckle and soothed Esca's cock with his tongue and his mind. Moving up, he added his other hand to Esca's shaft and kissed him, the slow deliberate penetration mimicking his possession of the man's ass.

"More." Esca groaned. "Faster."

"I don't want to hurt you." Despite his words, Ash eased a second oiled finger in alongside the first, and started to work them back and forth.

"And what if I want that?" Esca said. "What if I want to feel owned, possessed, and *sore*? What if I want to remember you fucking me hard when I'm sitting on that spaceship tomorrow?"

"How hard?" Ash's cock jerked and he fought the urge to come.

Esca's brown eyes were narrowed and full of lust. "As hard as I can take. I'm a big, tough soldier. I know you're being careful with me, but—"

Ash kissed him, shoving his tongue into Esca's mouth, adding a third finger and working him until his hips lifted and his cock filled out again.

"Gods, yes."

It was enough encouragement for Ash to draw back, grasp his cock and press the head against Esca's well-lubed ass.

"Do it." Esca growled. "Do me hard."

Ash pushed forward, gasping at the tightness of Esca's passage, each tiny gain a victory, each yielding, a mark of his right to possess this arrogant magnificent male, to own him as no other man ever would.

"Ah…" Ash paused to appreciate the sight of the last inch of his cock disappearing inside Esca. He looked down at the other man and held still.

"Hard enough for you?"

He was rewarded with a flicker of a smile. "You feel as big as my fist."

"And I haven't even started pounding into you yet."

"What are you waiting for?" Esca licked his lips and squeezed his own cock.

"I just wanted to appreciate the moment, to see you on your back, filled with my cock just as I've imagined you countless times."

"I've imagined it too."

Ash rocked his hips, watched Esca's expression tighten. "It's better than I dreamed."

"Then finish it. Fuck me. Make me yours."

Ash didn't need any more encouragement. He leaned into Esca and started to thrust, each jerk of his hips exploding a thousand sensations through his tightly encased cock and his mind. Esca's thoughts reached him too, became entwined and for a moment as he powered toward a climax, were indistinguishable from his. As he came, he even thought he could see those new neural connections being formed through the red haze of his closed eyes.

When he opened his eyes he lay against Esca's chest, one hand tangled in his lover's short dark hair. He eased his cock free and came up on one elbow to assess his mate.

'Shall we shower?"

"You don't want me to leave?"

Ash opened his eyes wide. "Without reciprocating?"

Esca went still. "You'd let me do that to you?"

"Yes." Ash rolled over and stood up, loved the way Esca's gaze rested on his nakedness. "We are supposed to be mated."

"But I always assumed—"

"That you were destined to be forever fucked and left wanting?" Ash opened the door into his lavish bathroom and put on the shower. "You don't have to fuck me." He stepped under the blissfully hot water and waited for Esca to join him. "If we add a female to our threesome, you could choose to only fuck her."

He opened his eyes as Esca's hand closed around his cock.

"Oh, I think I want you."

Ash smiled. "Then let's not waste any more time."

2

One planetary year later

"What's wrong? Are you in pain?"

Esca turned from his contemplation of the city lights to find Ash framed in the doorway of his suite.

"I'm fine." He surreptitiously moved to ease the cramp in his leg. "I was just thinking about tomorrow."

Ash sat beside him on the couch, his quiet presence always made Esca feel better. He wore his usual silk robe and his long pale hair was tied back at the nape of his neck. He smelled of the shower and of himself, an indefinable scent Esca still craved like a drug. His robe was tied so loosely that Esca could see his finely muscled torso, the long limbs and strong fingers that made sharing his bed so freking pleasurable.

Not that they'd been sharing much recently, what with Esca's injury and Ash's preoccupation with the affairs of the senate... That was probably his fault too.

After he'd gotten out of hospital and returned to the apartment, his lover had taken time off to care for him, putting up with his moods, his rages and his totally unreasonable demands. And now Ash was slammed with work.

"Are you sure you're fit enough to go on this mission?"

Esca's guilty thoughts about Ash dissipated, and he cast him an irritated glance. "Sure I am."

"You're certain?"

"You might be First Male, but you aren't my mother, or the military physician. Luckily, the latter declared me fit, so I'm going."

"Whether I think it's a wise decision or not."

"What are you going to do, stop me?"

"I could."

"And you know I'd never freking forgive you if you did."

"I'm concerned about your fitness."

"I get that." Esca stared out at the city. "I can't stay here forever. The accident was months ago. I've passed all the tests the military have thrown at me, I'm not in pain, I'm mentally competent and I'm bored witless here."

Ash didn't say anything his gaze fixed on the rapidly darkening horizon, too.

"Dammit, Ash."

"What?"

"You're determined to make this difficult for me, aren't you?"

"I'm well aware that the decisions I make in the Senate have caused this war to drag on, and—"

"—You don't like being reminded up close and personal of the cost of those decisions?" Esca gestured at his leg, which despite all his declarations to the contrary still hurt like frek. "I do my job. You can't protect me from everything."

"I know that you wouldn't be the extraordinary leader and tactician you are if you were any different. I just wish you were more careful sometimes."

"I'm a special ops soldier. I'm not paid to be careful."

Ash swung around to study him. "You were offered a promotion out of the field. Why didn't you take it?"

Esca took a long slow breath. "How the frek do you know about that?"

"I was informed by the military." Ash paused. "It would've been nice if you'd mentioned it to me yourself."

"Really, or did you tell them what you wanted to happen?" Esca glared at his companion. "Dammit, Ash."

"I didn't ask."

Esca's skeptical expression made Ash stiffen, and slam down his shields. "I've expressed my concern, you've told me it's irrelevant. I accept that. Have a successful trip." He rose from the couch. "Goodnight, *Second*."

Esca forced himself to remain still and seethe quietly. Even with their unique psychic link, sometimes Ash could be the devil to understand. He certainly didn't need the male who practically ran the Senate treating him like a little lost puppy. None of Ash's colleagues would believe their leader had a weakness like him. Sometimes he didn't believe it himself.

He resolutely stared out over the city. His bags were packed and he was going on the next mission. If he didn't go…

With a curse, he heaved himself upright and went through to Ash's rooms, not bothering to knock. His First Male was seated at his desk working, his expression absorbed. He looked older than his thirty-four years, more careworn and exhausted. Despite Ash's calm exterior, Esca knew better than anyone the tremendous strain his mate was under.

"You work too hard." Esca leaned against the door. There was no reply and the deliberate static in Ash's mind stopped Esca from communicating properly with him. "Ash."

Without turning, Ash finally replied. "There's an emergency vote coming up. I have to deal with it."

"*Ash*." Esca pushed through the psychic fog as hard as he could. "*I'm sorry*."

"As you so rightly put it, I'm not your mother. If anyone should be apologizing it should be me. I promised I'd never interfere with your career."

"You said you didn't." Esca looked up at the ceiling and then back down at the floor. He was so crap with words. "I behaved like an ass. We're mated. You have a right to be worried about me." He sucked in a breath. "It's just that if I don't go back now, I'm scared I'll never go back, and I'll be stuck behind a desk for the rest of my life."

Ash turned to look at him, his features a perfect mask, his smile the political one Esca hated. He shrugged. "Then go."

"What do you know about this mission that I don't?" Esca asked slowly.

"Nothing." Ash turned back to his screen, which now showed the floor of the Senate and the votes coming in. "I'm sure you'll be fine."

"Don't freking lie to me."

"It's not a matter of policy or actual knowledge." He sighed. "It's more a personal sense of disquiet that I didn't want to mention because you already think I'm overprotecting you."

"Like a premonition?"

"Exactly."

"And what is it you fear?"

"That this time you won't *come* back."

Esca exhaled like he'd been punched in the gut. "Great. Thanks. I appreciate your confidence in me."

"That's not what I meant." The screen flashed a warning and began to count down the seconds. Ash glanced back at it. "Esca —just let me attend to this vote, and—"

"Frek you."

Esca wrenched open the door and slammed it as physically shut as his psychic shields. The door to his suite was ajar, and his bags sat ready at the foot of the bed. He picked them up and headed for the elevator. If he stayed here any longer, Ash would seek him out, and he had nothing to say that wouldn't provoke another argument. Soldiers were a superstitious bunch, and the last thing he needed when he was already nervous about a mission was someone foretelling his death.

His own damned mate as well.

Frek him. Esca hoisted his bag onto his shoulder and stepped into the elevator. Whatever awaited him it had to be better than that.

"...AND the alliance troops are from Etrusca, a small militarized planet at the far end of our system. One thing to be aware of with this species is their aversion to psychics. Other than that, they have proved to be a most worthwhile fighting force."

Esca blinked hard and focused on the screen as the ships' captain brought him up to speed on the new mission.

"Why don't they like telepaths?"

His cousin Trenx stopped talking and stared at him. "I don't know why. Just don't be obvious about communicating telepathically in front of them, that's all. Are you feeling okay?"

"I'm fine. It's just a lot to take in." Esca sat up straight. "Where do you want my team?"

Trenx put up a map. "This is the military installation we're planning on obliterating, so we need as much upfront intel as you can get us. We're combining your team with the Etruscans to get the fullest coverage we can, but you're in overall command."

Esca studied the well-guarded facility set high in the mountains of the planet below them. "Not a problem." He rose from his chair.

"You're not planning on going on this one, are you?"

"Why not?" Esca could almost feel his hackles coming up.

"It's only an exploratory expedition. If it's successful, and depending what we find, we'll want you down there to lead the first strike." Trenx frowned. "Your team have worked with the Etruscans before, they won't mess up. Captain Jong's in command."

"She should do a fine job. What time are they off?"

Trenx consulted the screen. "In less than an hour."

"Then I'll go down and listen in on the briefing." Esca nodded at his cousin. "Thanks for the update."

Trenx finally smiled. "It's good to have you back."

Esca made his way down to the launch decks and was directed toward a small room where he could already hear his second-in-command speaking to the assembled team. She sounded extremely confident, and why shouldn't she? In his absence, she'd handled everything in a way that had made him proud.

And jealous as hell.

The whole room sprang to their feet as he appeared in the doorway.

"Sir!" Captain Jong saluted him. "Good to see you back."

He nodded, took a seat and gestured for her to continue. After a second, she did so, her delivery impeccable. He took a moment to check out the original members of his team and the new additions from Etrusca. There were about twenty of them in all, roughly half male and half female. He was so used to picking up other team members random thoughts that it was odd to have nothing coming back from half the room. How did they communicate in situations when they couldn't speak? Telepathy was invaluable to his team, and had saved their lives on more than one occasion. He'd have to ask Jong how they handled it.

As she drew to a close, Esca shifted in his seat, and she looked inquiringly at him.

"Is there anything you want to add, Major?"

He stood and faced the room. "Just that I'd like to welcome the Etruscan members of our combined force."

One of his first team members stood and saluted him. "Will you be leading us today, sir?"

"I don't see any need. Captain Jong is capable of carrying out a surveillance operation such as this in her sleep."

There were a few smiles, and he thought he detected a hint of relief in his second-in-command. "I will be coming on the next mission. I look forward to seeing how much you have improved under Captain Jong's excellent leadership."

He stood back to allow the soldiers to file past him, sharing a smile with those he knew, and a nod with the new team members. Jong waited until they'd all left before approaching him.

"If you wish to take command, sir, I'm—"

He held up his hand. "You'll do fine, Captain. I have every confidence in you." He looked out of the door. "I only see nine Etruscans. I thought there were ten."

"There's one more, sir, but she's not usually invited to the meetings." Jong grimaced. "I have to brief her separately. She's not considered equal to the others."

"What the hell does that mean?"

"They won't sit with her, sir." Jong shrugged. "I've tried but they just won't."

"Is she infectious or something?"

"No, she's a telepath."

"Ah." Esca nodded. "Captain Trenx said something about that to me earlier."

"She's the most useful member of the team. She only has basic skills, but I can at least communicate directly with her." Jong hesitated. "However, it's hard for her to get her team leader to listen."

"Which one is he?"

"Captain Wassain."

Esca studied the soldier who was busy suiting up for the mission. He looked like a pompous ass. "There's no point talking to him about the stupidity of this right before an operation. Let me know whether you encounter any issues. I'll keep an eye on the situation when I go out with you later."

"Thank you sir." She saluted him. "I'm really glad you're back, Major. We were all beginning to wonder—"

He cut her off with the professional smile he'd learned from Ash. "Whether I'd make it? Having your kneecap and thighbone shattered into a hundred pieces takes time to fix. I'm recovered now."

"I'm glad to hear it." She lowered her voice. "It's tough at the top."

"From all reports, you not only survived but thrived in command, Captain."

She flushed. "Thank you, sir. I'd better go and get ready."

"Good luck, Captain."

He nodded and watched her stride confidently away. If Ash's gloomy prediction did come true and he didn't survive the mission at least he'd be leaving his team in excellent hands...

Pushing such negativity aside, he took the elevator back up to the command center and settled in to watch the progress of the raid.

"No, DAMMIT—DON'T" Esca realized he was shouting at the screen and that Trenx was giving him dubious looks. He pointed at the display. "Those Etruscan idiots are far too close. Even a blind geriatric could spot them."

Trenx pointed to his mouth. "Tell Jong, don't scream at me."

"Sorry." Esca clicked on his mike. "Jong, are you receiving me?"

A burst of gunfire made him wince. Behind it he could just

make out the sound of Jong's voice issuing crisp, succinct commands.

"I've got it, Major."

"Good."

"We're coming back in."

"Even better."

Esca took off his headset and dropped it on the console. Pushing back his chair, he nodded at Trenx and his second-in-command, and headed back down to the launch deck to await the return of his team and the debriefing.

He didn't have long to wait until the men and women started to filter in from the landing craft. Captain Jong and the Etruscan leader were the last to appear and were arguing intensely. Esca stopped them from entering the debriefing room and pulled them to one side.

"What's going on?"

Captain Wassain saluted. "Nothing, Major."

Esca turned to Jong and raised an eyebrow. "Captain?"

"Sir, he left one of the team down on the surface."

"*What?*"

Wassain shrugged. "As I said, it's not important. She knew the risk. She also knows we won't recover her."

Jong stepped forward. "We don't leave anyone behind, Captain."

"Private Lang knows the deal. She's considered natural wastage and totally expendable."

"But—"

Esca held up his hand. "Jong, which team member is he referring to?"

"Private Lang. Their telepath."

"As I said, natural wastage." Wassain turned to Esca. "Can we get on with the debriefing? My team fucked up and I'd like to know why. It was probably something to do with that scum we left behind."

"By scum you mean your telepath?" Esca pointed behind him. "You do realize that every single member of my team who just saved your *ass* is a telepath?"

Wassain's face turned as red as his regimental facings. "I am aware of that, sir."

"And yet you don't consider your own team member to be worth *saving?*"

Wassain didn't answer, and stared steadily ahead. Esca motioned to Jong. "Take the team through what happened and send me a full report."

"Yes, Major." Captain Jong saluted and headed toward the door.

Wassain went to follow her and Esca blocked his path. "Not you. You're going to tell me exactly where you left Private Lang."

"I don't like this." Trenx glowered at Esca. "Ash will have my head."

"Ash can go frek himself." Esca continued to dress and arm himself. "It's quite simple. I'll take Wassain and find Private Lang. If she's still alive, we'll rendezvous with you at the original pick up site, and you can blast the facility to kingdom come from space. You have the capability."

"You're too valuable."

"I'm a *soldier*, not a senator's pet."

Trenx swung around in his chair. "I should inform Ash."

"Why? You know he doesn't interfere with my job." Esca shoved another grenade in his belt. "By the time you've gone bleating to him, I'll be safely onboard again, and you'll look like an idiot."

Trenx raised his hands. "Fine. You're higher ranked than me. Do what the frek you like."

"Thank you." Esca checked the time. "Ask Jong to send me that report. I'll listen to it as we approach the surface and make sure I don't repeat the same mistakes."

ESCA LANDED the shuttle and reset the controls to automatically pilot the vehicle back to the ship after they'd disembarked. Captain Wassain watched him, his expression deeply unhappy.

"This isn't necessary, Major. My superiors are not going to like it."

Esca stared him down. "I don't give a damn what your superiors think. This is my team and Private Lang is a member of it. No one gets left behind on my watch."

"I've given you her last coordinates, sir. Can't we just extract her from there?"

"You don't think we've tried that remotely? She's obviously been moved into the facility. No, Captain, you're not sitting safely on this shuttle when one of your soldiers is in danger. You're coming with me, and that's an order."

"And what if I refuse?" Wassain was sweating now, his gaze anywhere but on Esca's.

"Then I'll have you court-marshaled."

"My superiors would never uphold such a conviction."

"Then I'll kill you myself." Esca unbuckled his harness and pointed at the door. "Get out of your seat, exit this shuttle and proceed with me to the co-ordinates." He opened the exterior hatch and turned to flick on the command sequence for relaunch. "*Now*, Captain."

He waited another moment and then followed Wassain out of the shuttle. The outside temperature was warm and humid, and the air tasted slightly metallic. He checked his weapons, aware of the voice of the autopilot counting down the seconds behind him. Wassain suddenly stopped and swung around to face him.

"This is stupid. Private Lang isn't worth our lives."

"She's certainly worth yours." Esca aimed his weapon at the coward's heart. "Get moving."

Wassain lowered his head and charged for the rapidly closing door of the shuttle. Esca stepped forward and body checked him, bringing them both to the ground. His injured leg crumpled beneath him and he ended up underneath Wassain. Within a second, Wassain brought his weapon down on Esca's unprotected head, stars exploded, and he knew no more.

3

———————

Private Soreya Lang closed her eyes and leaned back against the rough wall of her cell. She might as well get comfortable. The guards had finally left and she had time to assess the new damage to her body. They weren't complete idiots. They'd been careful not to break anything, but she ached all over, and her head was throbbing from the tests their so-called scientist had run on her.

It was obvious the facility guards had strong opinions on females in the military and considered it their duty to show her why she should've stayed home. She shivered and carefully drew her knees up to her chest. If no one took any notice of the ransom demand they'd sent to the ship, she could count on their behavior deteriorating. And no one would take any notice. She was a Class Six, the scum of the Etruscan universe. They'd be more likely to rescue a pet fish than her.

So, she was going to die horribly.

A commotion outside her locked door made her heart race and she skittered further along the wall into the corner. If she were going to be executed, she'd take as many of them down with her as she could. She braced herself as the door opened and something was thrown in.

Dead bodies for dinner?

She wouldn't put it past them. Except that this one groaned. She remained where she was as the male uncurled from his fetal position and came up on one elbow.

"Freking assholes!"

In the dim lighting she noticed he wore the uniform of the Pavlovan military and that he was a big guy. Like all the Pavlovan males his size and telepathic abilities made her instantly wary.

He groaned and rolled onto his side, his head turned toward her dark corner.

"Private Lang?"

His voice was low and rough and carried an unmistakable air of authority. She immediately wanted to snap to attention and salute him.

"I'm Esca." And then his voice added in her head. "*I've come to get you out.*"

"*By getting yourself captured?*"

"*That wasn't part of my original plan. That idiot Wassain knocked me out, bolted like a scared wrazen back to the shuttle, and left me for dead.*"

"*That's because you're a telepath. He believes you have no value.*"

"*I got that.*" He sighed. "*Damn.*"

She cleared her throat and spoke out loud. "They sent a ransom note to the ship earlier. I don't expect it will do much good."

He slowly sat up and inched backward toward the nearest wall. Echoes of his pain floated through Soreya's mind.

"Are you injured?"

"My leg."

"Do you want some water?"

"Yes, if there is some."

She came out of her corner and crawled over to the far wall where the guards had left her rations. The water bottle was still almost full. Despite her reservations as to his size, she crouched down beside him and handed him the container.

"Help yourself."

He sipped a little and then a little more and then gave it back to her.

"Thanks."

His shoulder bumped against hers and she jumped. It was intoxicating to be so close to a male empath, to hear the rhythm of his thoughts moving alongside her own. And despite, his ordeal, he even smelled good. She had the absurd desire to press her face against the crook of his neck and simply inhale him.

Maybe her government had a point about keeping male and female telepaths strictly apart. She felt quite unlike herself, all needy and—

"You're hurting, too."

She glanced up at him and then wished she hadn't. This close, his eyes were a deep warm brown, his military short black hair fighting a curl and his hard mouth was...

"I can help you with that."

He reached for her hand and she snatched it away.

"What's wrong?" he hesitated. *"Did those bastards touch you, hurt you?"*

She shrugged which brought her even closer into his shoulder. *"Just a little welcome to our facility party. I don't think they appreciate female soldiers or telepaths."*

He reclaimed her hand. *"Then let's do our best to heal each other."*

"I don't know how."

"It's easy. Just let down your shields a little."

She looked at him. *"Easy? To do that?"*

He squeezed her hand. *"I forgot you don't live in a very tolerant society. Your shields are extraordinary. Even most telepaths wouldn't get anything out of you without your permission."*

"*Thank you.*" She concentrated very hard and felt his mind flow into hers. She'd always hated leaving herself vulnerable. The shock of his intrusion was like a jolt of caffeine. "*Oh.*"

"*Can you feed it back to me?*"

She concentrated again, and felt him respond in an infinite loop of healing. Within a few moments, her headache dissipated, as did the ache in her kidneys and ribs.

"*Better?*"

"Yes, sir." she eased her hand away. "Thank you, sir."

"Esca will do fine."

"But you're an officer."

"Captain Jong is in charge of this operation." He shifted position as though to test the strength in his leg. "I'm still technically on leave."

"Which means no one will come after us."

"*I've arranged a pick up in thirty-six Pavlovan hours. All we have to do is get out of here and meet the shuttle.*" He sighed. "*Of course I didn't expect Wassain to run off and leave me inside the facility as opposed to breaking my way in.*"

Soreya smiled for the first time. "*I can get us out.*"

"*Then one wonders why the hell you're still sitting here.*"

She glanced up at him. "*Because there was nowhere for me to run.*"

He shifted closer until his upper body was aligned with hers against the wall. "*Wassain said you were considered natural wastage. I told him where to stuff it.*"

"*I bet he took that well.*"

"*So well that when I get back I'm going to either kill him with my bare hands, or have him court-marshaled.*"

The cold fury in his words made Soreya shiver and yet she wasn't afraid of him. It was the first time anyone had stood up for her since her mother was taken. She fought to get her mind back onto the practical.

"If they are consistent, the guards check in about every two hours. I can create a diversion that will fool them long enough for us to get away."

"Then do it, Lang."

She nodded and walked over to the door. There was no sound from outside but the cell doors were thick so that could be deceptive.

Esca's deep voice resonated in her head. *"I can sense life forms through their thought patterns. There's no one out there."*

She focused on the wall closest to the door, and placed her palm on it. Closing her eyes she allowed her mind to follow the pulses of energy, sorting them into their correct forms and identifying the systems she needed.

"Are you ready, sir?"

He rose to his feet and came to stand beside her. Upright he loomed over her.

"What can I do?"

"Do you have a map of the interior of the facility?" He sent it to her telepathically. "Thanks. Can you keep an eye on our escape route while I deal with the security system?"

"Absolutely, Lang."

She found the five separate sources she needed to control and pushed power into them. "Then let's go."

The door opened without a sound, and she looked quickly up and down the hallway. There was no sign of any guards, and the alarms were silent. That would change, but they'd have to deal with it.

"Go right." He tapped her shoulder and they set out, her hand trailing along the wall, keeping contact with the power so that she could manipulate it at will. *"Guard on the other side of this door. I'll get him."*

The door clicked open as they approached, and the man

leaning against it on the other side fell backward. Before he even hit the ground Esca was on him. The snap of a broken neck echoed in the silent hall. He took the guard's weapons, and put him behind the door before locking it again.

"*Go.*"

She didn't need to be told twice, and set off again, her heart pumping hard in her chest, her awareness split between the delicate task of managing the facilities complex security systems and the sheer physicality of the male beside her.

"*Four guards approaching down the left hallway.*"

"*I'm blocking that entrance.*"

"*We need to turn at some point.*"

She pictured the map. "*Two hallways down.*"

He stiffened as the faint wail of sirens permeated the hall-way. "*What the hell is that?*"

"*Alarms going off in sector one to draw them away from us.*" She blinked at the myriad of tasks requiring her attention in her mind. "*I'm working on opening the last set of doors to the exterior courtyard. If we get through those, we're almost clear.*"

"*Go for it.*"

He locked and loaded the weapon and ran alongside her, his breathing untroubled, his gaze ranging the entire area. They turned left and kept running.

"*Here.*"

"*Get down.*"

She gasped as he shoved her to one side and raised his weapon, the crack of the shot was loud in the enclosed space and a single guard fell in front of her. She scrambled over the body and almost fell. Esca grabbed her arm and hauled her upright and onward.

"*Can't...silence these, but I've set them all off to give us more time.*"

As he pushed the door open, the ear-splitting wail of a siren pierced the night sky, swiftly followed by what sounded like a thousand others. He kept hold of her elbow, guiding her across the bleak ditch between the tall outer walls, boosting her up and over the first and then the second. She fell on her face, ate soft dirt and didn't care.

"Where now?"

"Up toward the mountains."

They started to climb. Below them the compound was in chaos, lights flashing, sirens blaring and men swarming all over like ants. Eventually, her breathing became as ragged as the rocky landscape and she started to slow. He drew to a halt and grinned down at her.

"Good work, Lang. That's one hell of a skill set you have there."

"It's the only reason the military tolerates me."

He nodded, his expression once again all business. "We have to keep moving. I'm pretty damn sure they'll regroup and come after us."

She followed behind him, aware of the threat at her back and more than willing to use all her strength to get as far away from the facility as possible. He took a circuitous path but it was always up. The air around them grew colder and she had to focus on her breathing.

He stopped so suddenly she bumped into the back of him.

"We'll rest here."

"I can keep going, sir."

"I can't." He limped over to an overhanging rock, picked up a fallen tree branch and thrust it into the shadows. "This will give us some shelter."

She followed him, her feet stumbling over the fallen rocks and gravel and sank down beside him. He grimaced as her knee collided with his thigh.

"Sorry, sir."

"It's Esca, and it's okay. It's an old injury which doesn't take well to the cold."

"Perhaps we could try that healing thing again."

"We will once we've had some water and a few rations." He brought out their meager supplies. "I'll try and contact the ship."

"From here?"

"It's unlikely, but it can't hurt to try. If I know Trenx and Captain Jong, they'll already be looking out for us on the planet surface."

"Even if Captain Wassain says you're dead?"

His smile was predatory. "One of Jong's strengths as a telepath is the ability to detect meershit. She'll not believe I'm dead until she's personally recovered my corpse."

She sensed him communicating, but he got no response.

"Would it help if I boosted your signal?"

He glanced down at her. "You're full of surprises, Lang, aren't you?"

"I don't know, sir. I've never had the chance to compare myself to other telepaths. We're kept strictly apart." Which she'd started to understand considering the devastating effect he was having on her.

"They don't let you mix?"

"No, sir. There are hardly any of us, and we're almost all female. Most males are exterminated at birth or as soon as they are identified." His silence made her hurry on. "It certainly makes it hard to understand ones abilities and what is normal and what isn't."

"So these gifts are innate?"

"Most of them." She swallowed hard. "My mother taught me a lot, mainly how to conceal them."

"She must be very proud of you."

"I don't know about that, sir. They executed her when I was ten for perverting a minor."

"You."

"Yes, sir."

"That's appalling."

"That's Etrusca." She forced a smile. "Do you want to try it then sir?"

ESCA STUDIED Private Lang's upturned face. She had blue grey eyes, brown hair and a small prim mouth, which gave her the look of a rather severe doll. Not that he cared about the exterior packaging. His senses were still reeling from the extraordinary power of her psyche, of the sense that her abilities called to him alone. The nearest he'd ever had to such an intense reaction was to Ash.

And that, in this particular set of circumstances, was both horrifying and wonderful. He wanted to die for her. He wanted to hold her close, and never let her go. She'd never met another male telepath up close and personal, and had no idea what he might be imagining, let alone deciding about her mating prospects.

Damn.

He had to get her back on the ship. There was no option for failure. Once she was safe, he'd deal with the matter of getting her naked and acquainted with him at a more reasonable pace.

"Let's try it."

He allowed his mind to blend with hers. It wasn't exactly difficult when he'd started to crave the contact like a drug. Her unique psychic signature shot through him and he freking shook with it. Faintly, right on the edge of his senses he felt Trenx. Grabbing Lang's hand he squeezed it hard and did the equivalent of a telepathic bellow. *"Coming up mountain to rendezvous spot. Need provisions and weapons. Will contact you when reach designated drop zone area."*

He disengaged, felt Lang pull away too, and realized he was still holding her hand. He wanted to bring it to his mouth and plant a kiss on her palm, draw each of her fingers into his mouth and show her exactly how he liked his dick to be sucked.

"Sir?"

He glanced down at her confused face, and grimaced at the tiredness and strain behind her eyes.

"I'm not sure if we reached him, but I think we did. We'll find out when we get closer to the top of this ridge." He kissed her cold nose. "Have some more water and we'll get going."

She didn't move, her gaze fixed on his mouth. He leaned in and brushed his lips over hers, heard her sharp intake of breath. "Lang?"

Her tongue flicked over her lower lip and he was lost. He joined his mouth with hers, the shock of the heat inside a sharp contrast to the cold. His cock kicked up in his pants. She didn't hesitate to kiss him back, and for him that was it. Confirmation that she was the one—that he had to have her and bring her home safely so that Ash could have her too.

But first, he had to save their asses.

He reluctantly pulled away. "I apologize, Lang, that was out of order."

She wiped her mouth and struggled to her feet. ""It's all right, sir. You're not the first superior officer who's ignored protocol and pulled rank on me."

He caught her elbow. "That's not what this is about, and you know it. When we get back on the ship—"

"You'll expect me to keep my mouth shut." She shoved the water container back in his hand. "I get it, sir."

She crawled out of the shelter and walked over to the side of the trail. "There are lights down below. I think they've found us."

Esca came to join her, the complications of mating lost in the reality of pursuit. "Let's get moving."

As they struggled up the increasingly treacherous path, Esca checked back on Lang but she appeared to be going strong. If anything, he was likely to be the problem, his leg didn't like the terrain at all and the bone-grinding ache was growing worse with every step.

"Someone's trying to contact you, sir."

Lang in his head, her voice devoid of emotion. He kept moving, but allowed her access to his mind, her power strengthening the fragile link.

"Cave at coordinates three, point five, point seven nine. Now equipped. Rest up and move onto drop zone at 05 hundred hours. Trenx out."

"Roger that."

Esca dragged the map to the front of his brain and fixed the position of the cave, aware that Lang was doing the same. He altered course and kept moving up, Wisps of snow brushed his cold face and the wind cut like the sharpest laser.

The entrance to the cave was extremely hard to see. If Trenx or his team had been in the area there was now no sign of them.

"Up there, sir."

Lang pointed at a slightly uneven shadow higher on the bleak rock face wall. Once he saw it, he knew she was right. He moved past her, his weapon at the ready. "Let's go."

The entrance was narrow and involved sliding between several upright rocks and then sideways between two massive horizontal slabs into what felt like a surprisingly warm and expansive space. There was a faint green glow to his left. He dug the light source out of the gravelly pit and flicked the power switch to full. Light flashed on the back of the cave where a neat pile of stores had been placed.

"Thank the Gods." Esca muttered. "Or more likely, thank Captain Jong."

There were two thin heat-preserving blankets, basic rations, and a small arsenal of weapons. Esca spread one of the blankets over the stone floor and gestured at Lang.

"Sit on this so you won't freeze your ass off. We'll divide the weapons, set up a perimeter alarm, eat, heal, and then try to sleep. Any questions?"

"No sir." She subsided onto the blanket beside him and he realized she was shivering. He handed her a gun. "Are you familiar with this weapon?"

"Yes."

"Then make sure it's fully charged, and help yourself to anything else Jong left us." He armed himself to his satisfaction and felt much better. "I'll go and set the traps and charges around the cave while you take care of the entranceway."

"Yes sir."

He had to grit his teeth to get off the floor without his leg giving way. "I'll be back. I'll let you know when I'm coming in."

She nodded, her gaze on the gun he'd given her, her competent hands checking it over in a way that made him want to fuck her even more. Frek, his timing was terrible as were his basic urges. Why hadn't she met Ash first? He was the diplomat. He'd know just how to handle her.

He pulled on the extra warm jacket Jong had left him and headed outside. It didn't take long to set the charges and the trip alarms. In the silence of the mountain he could hear the pursuit below. They were making no effort to keep quiet, their voices loud, and their hunting dogs even louder. He wondered if they were stopping to make camp. Hopefully the storm would slow them down enough to make escape possible.

It damn well had to.

Esca turned back to view the cave. From here there was no sign of habitation or disturbance. He just prayed that none of the hunting party knew of its existence, and could lead the soldiers right to them. Even if that happened, he'd take down as many of them as he could before he surrendered Private Lang to anyone. Not that she'd be sitting idly by twirling her hair. He reckoned she'd be right alongside him matching him kill for kill.

What a female.

He just remembered to let her know he was coming back before he stepped inside the cave and into her raised weapon. He maneuvered awkwardly through the obstacles to the space behind. In the soft glow of the green light, he noticed a long slab of rock propped up against the wall. He hefted it up and slid it sideways, all but closing the gap to the outside world.

"Lang?"

She was sitting on the blanket, her knees drawn up to her chin and her arms wrapped around them.

"Yes, sir?"

"Break out those rations."

DAMN HIM. Soreya rubbed at her lips where the sensation of his kiss still lingered. She'd been kissed before, but never with such soul-baring intensity. If he hadn't drawn back she would've been climbing him like a tree and begging him to fuck her. Was this why the Etruscan government kept telepaths apart? She hadn't tried to leap on any of the other male team members from Pavlovan. But then none of them had kissed her...

"Lang?"

She stared at him as he shook the snow from his thick dark hair. "What?"

"Rations?"

Color rushed to her face and she bent her head over the box of supplies to hide her confusion.

"There's plenty here, sir." She spread the packets out on the blanket. "Not that it makes much difference what you pick, they all taste the same."

He sat down next to her, suddenly making the available space feel small.

"Give me your hand."

She obeyed before she thought it through and watched as her small hand disappeared inside his larger one. The now familiar heat of his healing power reached her and she tried to relax and send it back to him. She sensed he was in considerable pain and for some reason, she wanted desperately to fix that for him, to soothe him with her hands, her mouth her body...

"Lang, that isn't helping." he murmured.

"What isn't, sir?"

"What you're thinking."

She tried to pull her hand away, but he wouldn't let go.

"There is something I wanted to ask you, sir."

"Go ahead."

"If we are likely to be captured alive, will you kill me first? Knowing their opinion of females I doubt I'd get away with just being shot in the head."

He stirred beside her. "If they capture you, Lang, I'll already be dead. I'll do anything to keep you alive."

The sincerity in his voice made her throat tighten with long suppressed emotion. "Thank you, sir, but will you promise anyway?"

"Yes."

She managed to pull away. "Now what can I give you to eat?"

"Lang."

She raised her head and found him staring at her. "What?"

"You are a remarkable female."

She sat back next to him and waited until he started eating and followed suit.

"How is your leg?"

"Bearing up."

She chewed in silence for a while, and then leaned back

against the hardness of the wall to contemplate the shadows of the cave.

"Hold up." He wrapped an arm around her shoulders. "Less stress on your back."

She didn't protest and gradually found herself turning into his warmth and greedily inhaling his scent. Was this how it had been for her mother? This desperate need to be understood—to be recognized as having worth by another telepath?

"I think my father must've been a telepath."

"Considering your gifts, I'd assume he was."

"I never met him. He was from off—planet."

"Which might explain your particular talents." He shifted slightly toward her. "I've never met another telepath who can manipulate the information stream like you can. Captain Jong said that you only had the basic skills necessary to communicate."

"I have good shields. Sometimes our government sets traps using other telepaths. I always had to be careful."

He sighed. "And now after all your caution, you're stuck with me in a cave on the side of a mountain with a fifty-fifty chance that I'll get you killed."

"Fifty percent is better than it was before you arrived. Wassain left me for dead."

"Me too." His soft laugh brushed over her skin like the finest silk. "Your optimism amazes me. I'm sitting here full of regrets for all the stupid shit I haven't accomplished in my life."

"You don't think we're going to survive?" She twisted around to stare into his eyes. "Now you've got me thinking of all the things I regret too."

"Sorry Lang."

She kept staring at him as the truth of his words sunk in. What would she regret? She'd had to live so cautiously, and so carefully just to stay alive, and it had brought her here anyway and risked another man's life. She let out a long shuddering breath.

"There is something I'd regret."

"What's that?"

"Not kissing you again."

He went still. "Lang, if I kiss you, I'm not going to want to stop there."

Heat coalesced low in her belly. "Do you think I'd want you to stop?"

With a strangled sound, he picked her up and sat her on his lap so that she straddled him. His mouth descended and then there was nothing in her world except him, his taste, his tongue, and the thump of his heart and harried breathing. She shoved one hand in his hair and held on, her body moving against the hard swell of his cock and his broad muscled chest.

"Oh Gods…" She moaned as she started to come just from the friction and the overpowering need of his desire flooding through all her senses. He pressed his hand against her ass pushing her into the roll of his hips and the rod of his cock.

"I want you."

"Yes," He groaned against her lips. "Please."

She attacked the waistband of his pants, ignoring his sudden intake of breath as she unzipped him and stared at his standard issue black underwear. He was so aroused his cock was already pushing out of the top of his boxers. She bent her head and licked the exposed part, sucking it and the soaked fabric into her mouth. He tasted as raw and desperate as she felt.

His hand fisted in her hair. "I'll come if you keep doing that, and I want inside you."

She sat back and he helped her pull down her pants and underwear, shoving them off one leg to expose the important parts. While she struggled to push all the unnecessary fabric out of the way, he lifted his hips and pulled down his boxers to reveal the thick column of his cock.

"Oh..." Soreya breathed. "I wish..."

He lifted her again. "Next time. Just—"

She took him in, took more and more until she was full, and aching and rocking blindly against him as he continued to push upward. His fingers grazed her clit and she took even more, drowning in the sensations, in the rightness of having his body and his mind enmeshed with hers.

"Lang..."

She rose up and then pressed down again and he followed her rhythm, his mind as hot and needy as his cock, his thoughts so consumed with his delight in her that she felt like a goddess. She moved faster and his hands came to her hips to help. His mouth fused with hers as did his mind, and she was lost in him, in them, in whatever they were creating together.

Faster now, his thrusts joining her downward plunges keeping her filled and sending her to a dark hot place where nothing existed but their need for each other. She climaxed and he kept pumping into her, sending her even higher. Her nails dug into his shoulders and she bit down on his lip making him writhe beneath her and finally climax in endless, shuddering waves.

She didn't want to move ever again. She wanted to stay there, on his lap, his cock buried inside her forever. Would he feel the same? Was this how her mother had felt with her father? She'd told Soreya that she didn't regret a thing.

"Lang?" He whispered.

"Mmm?"

"Do you have another name?"

She raised her head to look into his eyes. "Yes, why?"

His smile was breathtaking. "I feel that we're at a point in our relationship when I should know what it is."

"Soreya."

"That's beautiful." He touched her cheek.

Unaccustomed tears rose in her throat and she pushed at his

chest to disentangle herself. "It's nothing special." She started to rearrange her clothing, and ended up sitting on the cold ground freezing her ass off as she struggled to put one foot back through her panties.

"Soreya."

"*What?*"

"I know this is difficult for you and my timing is lousy, but we *will* be discussing our relationship further, when we get back on the ship."

"If." She finally untangled her panties and pushed her foot through. "And this isn't a relationship it's just sex."

"You always have sex like that, do you?"

He was smiling openly at her now.

"Sure." She shrugged. "Don't you? I've gotten really good at faking it with my superior officers."

For a second he looked put out, and then a slight smile appeared again. "As I said, we'll discuss this when we get back on the ship." He patted the blanket next to him. "Now come and sit here and we'll attempt to get some sleep."

4

As she slept, she leaned closer in to him and he willingly took her weight. Just holding her made him feel good. Strike that, sex would be even better, but breathing her in was enough in the particular circumstances. He kissed the top of her head like a crazy besotted fool, and she murmured his name and put her hand on his chest.

He felt *complete*, like she was the missing piece in his head and his heart—the balance to his love for Ash, a female version of his male lover. Which, according to his people and traditions, was how it was meant to be. Who'd have thought he'd end up such a traditional old romantic? Ash would be amused.

Through his tiredness, Esca's mind was already busy working out the diplomatic tangle his wanting to bring an Etruscan into his country, an Etruscan who was considered scum by her own people. There had to be a way...

His alarm went off and he opened his eyes into the darkness of the cave. It was freking freezing. He gently shook his companion's arm.

"Lang? We've gotta get moving."

Her eyes flew open, and he registered the interesting mix of blue and grey.

"Yes, sir."

It didn't take them long to gather their stuff, arm their weapons and start for the landing zone. The rocks were slippery with ice and his breath froze on every exhale. It was deathly quiet out, no signs of the pursuit below.

That worried him.

"Shall we try and contact the ship, sir?"

He looked down at Lang, her face barely visible under the hood of her jacket.

"Yes."

She joined her superlative power to his and projected outward.

"Ten minutes." Trenx was much clearer now.

Esca judged the terrain ahead and projected their speed and current location. They should just make it if they kept a steady pace.

"Let's go." His leg was already bothering him but there was nothing he could do about that. The cold always made it worse.

The route was neither easy nor straightforward, but he kept on, Lang close behind him. As they approached the flat summit, the unsubtle roar of a descending troop transporter was already rattling the rocks. A glint of something metallic caught his eye. Before he could warn her, Lang was already going down and rolling into a ball.

"Esca, move it!"

He followed her as weapon fire streamed over where their heads had just been. She was crawling on her hands and knees, her face plastered with dust, her expression grim.

"One minute to landing, Major."

Lang grabbed his arm and pointed at a crevice in the rocks. *"We can get through there, and make a run for it as soon as the shuttle touches down."*

He nodded through the smoke and noise.

"We copy your situation, Major and will provide covering fire."

Captain Jong's calm voice filled his head and he sent up a quick prayer to the Gods.

"Did you get that, Lang?"

"Yes."

She didn't look back, all her attention on the descending shuttle and the deadly circle of guards closing in on it. As the shuttle landed, he closed in right behind her.

"Wait for Jong's signal and then run like hell."

The door opened, and Esca slapped Lang's shoulder. *"Run."*

He kept pace with her, desperately trying to protect her smaller body with his from the flying bullets, lasers and miscellaneous firepower. The shuttle door appeared through the smoke and he practically threw her in. She turned to help him up; and he took her hand, not stupid enough to deny that he needed assistance.

"No!"

She screamed and leapt over him, her foot glancing off his shoulder, knocking him sideways as a huge roaring pain scythed down his back. He felt her behind him, pushing and shoving him upward, her tiny frame staggering under his weight.

"Help me!"

He tried, but it was becoming increasingly difficult to avoid the roaring void of pain and the peacefulness of oblivion. But something about her voice, made him keep moving, keep breathing, keep striving...

Hard hands grabbed him and the door of the shuttle shut

with a thunk. The engines roared and the floor beneath him shuddered.

"We're away, sir."

"Lang?" He whispered as his vision started to fail. "Where the frek are you?"

She opened her eyes into an environment familiar to any soldier, a hospital bed, and frowned.

"Private Lang?" A female dressed in white sat down on the bed and smiled at her. "How are you feeling?"

"I'm good."

"I'm Mayek, the ship's physician. When they first brought you in you didn't look too good, you were covered in blood and unconscious."

She licked her dry lips. "It wasn't my blood. Is Esca okay?"

"He's asleep at the moment, but he's going to be fine."

"That's great."

"He's a very brave man."

Soreya managed a smile. "He is." She yawned and tried to cover her mouth. "I'm sorry."

"Don't be, you're suffering from exhaustion and mild hypothermia. The drip's in to give you proper nutrients and a dose of painkillers when necessary. It's intuitive so you shouldn't be in any pain. Use the call button if you need the nurse." The doctor patted her hand. "I'll pop in tomorrow morning and see how you are doing."

"Thanks."

After the doctor left, Soreya surveyed her small room, which contained only one bed. Where was Esca? She frowned as she sensed his growing restlessness, the way he was fighting the medication being steadily pumped into him. Without meaning to, she put her hand on the wall beside her bed and tuned into the workings of the ship.

She studied the schematic of the small sick bay. Three other rooms like hers, one other occupied. Dammit, she couldn't leave him in pain like that. She *needed* to touch him, to reassure herself that he was okay.

It took her only a second to figure out how to disconnect herself from the network and yet still appear to be there. She picked up the drip and held it over her head. There was no one in the hallway and it was only a few steps diagonally across the space to Esca's. She waited until the solitary nurse at the end of the hall walked away, closed her door silently behind her and let herself in his room.

He lay on his side, his face creased with pain, covers thrown off and his whole body shaking. With a soft sound, she hooked her drip up beside his and carefully got into bed with him, her back to his front.

"Lang."

"Yes. I'm here, now go to sleep, okay?"

He gathered her close and with a sigh relaxed against her. She sent him the healing power he'd taught her how to produce, felt it move inside him, calm him. Her eyes closed as she admitted that being with him calmed her too.

She woke later to the sound of running feet and agitated voices. It was the middle of the night and someone had obviously discovered she'd gone missing. It amused her how easily she could listen in on the other telepaths. They conversed with each other so freely. It wasn't a big ship. She wondered how long it would take them to work out where she'd gone.

When the door finally opened, she closed her eyes and pretended to be sleeping.

"Thank the Gods."

She recognized Dr. Mayek's relieved voice.

"How the hell did she get in here?" That deeper sound was the ship's captain, Trenx.

"I have no idea, but they look pretty comfortable together." She laughed softly. "I wondered why Major Esca was suddenly sleeping so well."

"It's not right. She shouldn't be with him, you know that."

Dr. Mayek sighed. "I know. I'll speak to her as soon as she wakes up, I promise."

"Can't you wake her?"

"Captain, believe it or not, for some reason, Major Esca is healing much faster with her support. If we force the issue, he might relapse."

"Then get her out of here as soon as you can."

"Understood."

The door closed again and Soreya opened her eyes. Why were they so worried about her being with Esca? Did they think she would contaminate him or something? She'd assumed being among telepaths would make her life better, but it seemed they were as suspicious of her motives as her own people.

"Lang?"

Esca's hand slid around to cup her breast.

"I'm here."

He tightened his grip on her, pulling her ass against the rising swell of his cock.

"You're supposed to be ill, sir."

His thumb flicked over her nipple and she sucked in a breath.

"I'm feeling better every minute."

He cupped her mound, rubbing her already slick sex and eager clit with strong, patient fingers. She shuddered as he drew her thigh up and back and slid his cock home.

"Mmm...nice." He kissed her neck. *"Don't have the energy to move. Just wanted to be inside you."*

It was strangely comforting, lying there, joined to him

feeling the pulse of his heartbeat through his buried cock, and his soft breathing in her ear. His fingers returned to her clit and he slowly circled and rubbed her tender sensitive flesh until she came for him in long shuddering waves before he joined her and fell back to sleep.

When she was certain he was asleep, she got up and took a quick shower, difficult when managing a drip. Pulling on her hospital gown she walked down to the main room and smiled at the nurse.

"Dr. Mayek wanted to talk to me. Is she around?"

"I'll call her."

She proffered her arm. "Can you take this out while we're waiting?"

Five minutes later she was sitting in the doctor's office and the door was closed. Not that it did much good in a ship full of telepaths who seemed to share every thought. She didn't think she'd ever relax enough to do that.

"Private Lang."

"You can call me Soreya if you want."

"Soreya, then." Dr. Mayek took a deep breath and then stared down at her folded hands. "When we recovered you from the planet surface we gave you a thorough physical examination. There were several bruises and abrasions on your skin."

"Well it was a bit of a bumpy ride."

"I understand that, but some of these...anomalies were consistent with physical abuse. We also recorded evidence of sexual intercourse and semen." She raised her head to look at Soreya. "I have to ask you—were you sexually abused either by the guards at the facility, or by Major Esca?"

"Abused?" Soreya searched the doctor's mind, but could find no trace of amusement. "The guards manhandled me in a deliberately crude way and Esca..." She paused. "Actually, I think I propositioned him."

Relief flashed across the doctor's mind. "I'm glad he didn't take advantage of his superior rank. That would've been quite unlike him."

"If any advantage was taken it was by me. I've never met an adult male telepath before. The temptation was too much to resist."

"That does change matters slightly, but he is still your superior officer. If you wish to press charges, I will support you."

"Why would I want to do that?" Soreya smiled. "It was my first and last opportunity to have sex with one of my own kind."

Dr. Mayek frowned. "There are no adult males in your society?"

"Not telepathic ones. We're not allowed to breed." Soreya stood up, her smile easy. "So, are we done here?"

A sense of bleakness settled over her as she strengthened her shields. Not that anyone on the ship thought she had any power or the potential to be useful. He'd be furious that she'd taken the blame for their sexual encounter. But whether Esca liked it or not, she was going to save his ass and his career. It was the least she could do. He'd given her more than she'd ever expected in her life.

"I'd like you to remain in sick bay until I've written my final report. We'll be arriving at Sub Station Rouge in the next day or so, where we will liaise with the Etruscan authorities."

"Oh great." Soreya pushed in her chair. "Is it okay if I go and sit with Esca?"

The doctor stood too. "To be honest, I wouldn't recommend it."

"Why?"

"It might just be better in the long run, don't you think?" Dr. Mayek patted her arm, her voice sympathetic. "He's from one of the first families in Pavlovan, and you're unlikely to see him again."

Soreya caught all the doctor wasn't saying. They thought she was infatuated with Esca, that she was a silly little girl on a hero-worshipping kick. Her stomach tightened with self-disgust. She really was just like her mother, an object of pity, a female who'd given up everything for the excitement of a quick fuck.

"Sure, whatever you think. You wouldn't want me getting all sentimental and emotional, would you? I'll be more than happy to go back to my sterile, home planet with this wonderful memory of Major Esca to sustain me through the rest of my barren and lonely life."

"Soreya…"

Pity.

She hated it. "Doc."

She escaped into her room and shut the door. Lying down on the bed, she stared up at the ceiling and allowed herself to cry.

Stupid.

What had she expected? That they'd suddenly see her true worth and rush to unite her with her one, true love?

"Private Lang?"

"Captain Trenx."

"Would you come to my quarters please?"

"Yes sir."

She hastily wiped her eyes. No doubt the good doctor had called in reinforcements to make sure their precious Major escaped unscathed from her unwanted crush on him. Her despised uniform was in the closet so she put it on. A security guard waited in the main sick bay and accompanied her through the upper floors of the ship to the captain's door. She knocked and went in.

He was sitting at his desk, his blond hair disheveled as though he'd been pulling it out, his uniform shirt open at the neck and his jacket discarded over a chair.

"Lang, come in." he pointed at the chair opposite him. "Sit down."

She saluted him and took the seat. She felt his mind press against hers in a tentative exploration.

"*Sir?*"

"We have a situation." He studied her face. "When we reach Sub Station Rouge we've been ordered to offload all the Etruscan members of our team, including you and Captain Wassain."

Soreya kept her expression neutral and after a second, he continued.

"We are insisting that Wassain is brought to justice for both his cowardly desertion of you, and his outright attack on Major Esca."

"They won't prosecute him for leaving me behind, sir."

He sighed. "So they've already told us."

"And I'm pretty sure that even if they do reprimand Captain Wassain publicly for his behavior toward Major Esca, they won't punish him."

"Because you are both telepaths."

"Exactly, sir." She hesitated. "I'm not sure why you're telling me this."

"Because I want you to know that whatever your government says, *my* government will do everything in its power to make sure that you are not...impacted in a negative way by these proceedings."

"Thank you, sir."

Didn't he understand that the moment the Etruscans got her back she was dead? She'd shown them up and forced a superior officer to behave badly in front of his allies. Sure, they'd probably wait until the Pavlovan ship left before they carried out her sentence, but she'd still be dead.

"Is there anything else, sir?"

"Yes. Dr, Mayek is concerned about you."

Inwardly Soreya sighed. "There's no need, sir. I'm completely recovered."

"She's not worried about your health." He cast her a quick glance. His mind felt as uncomfortable as he looked. "Major Esca saved your life and that can create a unique, if unrealistic bond between two people. I also understand that you aren't used to dealing with other telepaths. Connecting with a male of Major Esca's talents must've have been quite overwhelming for you."

Soreya set her jaw at his patronizing tone. "I'm fully aware of all this, sir. I'm not going to throw myself at him or anything."

"Good, because you're worth more than that."

"I am, sir?" She looked up into his very blue eyes. "I thought this little lecture was all about protecting Major Esca."

"Don't be sarcastic, Lang. I watched the security footage of the shuttle expedition to retrieve you and the major. *You* got him onto that ship. I have no idea how you managed it, but I'll never forget that." He leaned forward. "Neither will our nation. Major Esca's mate is a major political figure in our senate. If you need our assistance against your superiors, I'm sure our government would be grateful enough to put in a good word for you."

"Major Esca is mated?"

Captain Trenx nodded. "Yeah," he said gently. "For the last ten years or so."

From somewhere, Soreya summoned the ability to smile. "I doubt I'll need anything, but thanks for offering." She rose to her feet. "It *would* be helpful if you could get me off this ship without Wassain or the rest of the team seeing me. If you put me in with them, I might not make it to the barracks."

"Understood. We'll arrange a separate escort." He stood and held out his hand. "And don't worry, we'll do our best to protect you."

"Thank you, I appreciate that." She shook his hand. What else could she do? "I'd better get back to sick bay."

Major Esca was mated.

She followed the guard back along the narrow passageways, her thoughts in turmoil. What kind of 'relationship' had he been talking about? Was he the kind of male who kept another source of available ass on the side? Like her mother had been to her father, available, eager, and too in lust to demand a legal relationship.

She took off her uniform and lay on her bed. So her choices had narrowed to death or, what? She wouldn't want the gallant major to rescue her even if he wanted to. His ability to lie to her hurt far more than she'd anticipated. But she'd been so willing to be deceived...

"Lang?"

Damn him and the need in his voice. Damn him to hell. She wanted to go to him more than she wanted to breathe.

"Soreya?"

Not anymore. She sat up and glared at the door until it locked. Strengthening her shields she shut him out and forced herself to go to sleep. Tomorrow was going to be a busy day.

5

<hr>

"TRENX, WHERE IS SHE?" ESCA GLARED AT THE PROTESTING NURSE and the bleeping instruments as he pulled off his hospital jammies. "Get this out of my arm, or I'll rip it out."

"Esca, will you just calm down and wait for Mayek?" Trenx made soothing gestures with his hands. "Where do you think you're going anyway?"

"We've docked, haven't we?"

"Yeah. I'm waiting for the escort for Captain Wassain and the rest of the Etruscan team to arrive. Don't worry, I've arranged a separate escort for Private Lang."

"She's already *gone*, Trenx."

"You're delusional. She's in her room across the hall."

"She freking is not. How do you think we got out of that damn prison? She's a regular escape artist." Esca pulled his arm away from the nurse and grabbed hold of the tubing. "Take it out or it's coming out."

Trenx disappeared and came back a second later. 'She's not there."

"I told you so." He looked up as Dr. Mayek arrived. "Get this out of my arm, please. I have to get up."

"I don't think—"

Esca held out his arm. "I don't care what you think, that's an order."

She scowled at him but started to work on the shunt and tubing. "As your physician I don't recommend this. Are we clear on that?"

"Clear. I take full responsibility for my actions." Esca looked over at Trenx. "I need to find her."

Trenx ushered the nurse and Dr. Mayek out and closed the door. "I don't get it. If she's voluntarily gone back to the Etruscan army, why not let her go?" He hesitated. "Wouldn't it be kinder in the long run? Don't tell me you're infatuated with her as well? Dammit, Esca."

"I'm not infatuated with her. She's my mate."

Trenx snorted. "Funny. You obviously got hit on the head harder than I thought. She's a lightweight compared with you and Ash."

Esca buttoned up his shirt and stepped into his uniform pants. "You have no idea what you're talking about. If she'd wanted she could've taken control of this whole ship and sent it crashing into the nearest planet. At least at the moment, she's still alive. I'd know if she was dead." He swallowed hard. "The Gods know how long they'll keep her alive."

"There was no reason for her to run. I *told* her we would protect her to the best of our ability."

"Did you also tell her that she was infatuated with me?" Esca shook his head. "Of course you freking did. They'll execute her in a heartbeat, Trenx. That's what she's gone back to, and I don't understand why."

Inside him rage boiled and a sense of utter helplessness he'd never, experienced before. He wanted to find her and shake her until her teeth rattled and then fuck her until she begged for mercy and then…

"Hold up." Trenx paused. "I'm getting a message that she's being held at the embassy."

Esca put on his jacket. "Then we'll need to act fast. Call Ash and tell him to get the Pavlovan diplomat stationed here to meet us at the Etruscan embassy as a matter of urgency. Tell him I'll owe him one or whatever you need to get him to do what I ask. I'll need Dr, Mayek to come with me too."

Even if Lang didn't have enough faith in him to wait until he worked things out, he had to try and save her. And why should she believe him? She'd had no support from anyone during her entire life. It would've been nice to be consulted. Trenx had apparently decided he was to be left out of any decision-making concerning the Etruscans at all.

"When were you going to wake me up? Once we were gone from here?"

Trenx sighed. "I was trying to help."

"Then don't." Esca buckled on his weapon and reached for his hat. "Be ready to leave as soon as we get back. If this works, I don't want to hang around."

"LANG. STAND TO ATTENTION."

Soreya looked up at the guard framed in the doorway of her cell. It was the same one who'd taken her into military custody earlier that morning. She wondered what the guard would do if she didn't obey. If she was about to be executed she had no intention of making it easy on anybody.

"Lang, get up." Losing patience, the guard came forward and grabbed her around the neck jerking her head backward. Pain lanced through Soreya's ribs and back and she fought a groan.

"You're wanted. The Gods know why."

She allowed herself to be hauled to her feet, and was

marched out of the cell and along the short hallway of the secure wing. A moment later they were in the plush surroundings of the Etruscan embassy, which was a whole lot more welcoming. There was an open door to the left of the vast hall and she was steered through that. She stopped walking so abruptly that the guard behind her shoved her forward and she almost fell.

"It is necessary for Private Lang to be secured like that?"

She closed her eyes against the cold sound of Esca's clipped voice.

"She is in our custody, Major. It is customary for prisoners to be restrained for the safety of those around them."

"Private Lang doesn't look capable of hurting a fly, Ambassador Carver." A small white-haired woman stepped in front of Esca and smiled at the Etruscan diplomat. "Perhaps we might offer her a chair?"

Miraculously, a chair was produced, and Soreya was allowed to sit, her handcuffed wrists on her lap, her head lowered so that she didn't have to look into anyone's eyes. It didn't make any difference though. She was still far too aware of Esca's furious silence ringing in her head.

"As we were discussing, our nation would like to extend our thanks to Private Lang for saving the life of one of the members of our most prominent families." The female diplomat smiled at her.

"You may certainly do that, Madame Cara."

"But there is more. We would like to offer her the opportunity to share her unique telepathic skill set with our youth."

"I beg your pardon?" Ambassador Carver's faint smile disappeared. "You want to take her back to Pavlovan? But—"

"It would perhaps cancel out the *appalling* behavior of Captain Wassain toward his teammates and commanding officer." The female diplomat sat forward. "If you made this gesture of goodwill toward our nation by allowing us to learn from Private Lang, we would be prepared to drop all charges against

Captain Wassain and will not bring the matter before the alliance nations." She paused. "I'm sure you wouldn't want your allies to think your military is actively hostile to telepaths and allows its officer to disobey direct orders?"

Soreya blinked slowly as she tried to understand what the hell was going on. Were the Pavlovans really making all this effort just to save her? She straightened and bit her lip at the pain.

Esca bent forward and whispered something into his diplomat's ear.

"Perhaps while you and I discuss this matter, Ambassador, Dr. Mayek could check in with Private Lang? She needs to complete her record of care."

Ambassador Carver rose. "As long as there is a guard on the door, Dr. Mayek may examine her. Please come into my private study, Ambassador so that we can explore this delicate matter further."

As soon as the door closed behind the diplomats, Dr, Mayek came to kneel at Soreya's feet.

"What's wrong with her?" Esca's voice from the other side of the room.

"Bruised ribs and a battered face."

Aware of the guard by the door, Soreya tried to smile. "I fell against the door of my cell. It was my fault entirely."

"Like hell it was." Esca growled in her head and the whole structure of the room rocked.

Ouch.

She stared straight ahead as Dr. Mayek worked her magic with the judicious application of nano packs on her skin. The relief was immediate and she began to breathe less cautiously.

"Thanks."

Dr. Mayek squeezed her knee and got to her feet. "Hopefully, I'll see you later." She went to the door and engaged the guard in conversation, effectively blocking his view of Soreya and Esca who had remained propping up the wall. She watched his booted feet come over and swallowed hard.

"You shouldn't be up yet, sir."

"I'm aware of that, Lang. Unfortunately, I had no choice."

"I didn't expect you to come after me."

"I have to admit that I didn't think certain death at the hands of your own people was preferable to one meaningful conversation with me. Obviously, I miscalculated."

She raised her chin. "I'm not that stupid. I went to the refuge. They called the military police on me."

He swung around, his brown eyes searching, and she stumbled on. *"Walking away from you was the hardest thing I've ever had to do in my life."*

"Then for frek's sake why—"

The door opened and the Pavlovan ambassador came in.

"Private Lang? It's all settled. In return for us dropping charges against Captain Wassain, you are to be loaned to our university for a year for 'research purposes'. Are you willing to agree to this?"

Soreya stood up. "In exchange for my life? Yes, I certainly am." She glanced up at Esca's unsmiling face. "That is, if Major Esca agrees."

"Agrees? It was all his idea." The ambassador kissed Soreya's cheek. "He's a very determined man when he wants to be." She raised her voice. "Will someone take these restraints off Private Lang? She needs to be going."

On the ride back to the ship, Esca didn't speak to her at all. He spent most of his time answering Dr. Mayek's concerned questions and ignoring her advice for him to report back to sickbay as soon as they returned. Eventually even the good doctor gave up nagging and relapsed into silence, her gaze shifting between Soreya and the major, and her thoughts full of speculation.

Captain Trenx met them at the entrance to the space ship.

"We're ready to leave."

"Good." Esca nodded at the captain and at Dr. Mayek. "Come along, Private Lang."

"But—"

Esca slammed Trenx up against the wall. "Shut the frek up, *cousin*, and get this ship moving. I'll deal with Private Lang."

Soreya didn't protest as he marched her along to the officer's quarters and into his small cabin. She was too tired to think, let alone argue. He shut the door and she leaned back against it as he turned around.

"Turn off all security feeds and isolate this cabin."

"You should lie down, Major."

"Turn them freking off. I know you have the capability." He slammed a hand against the door above her head, leaned in and kissed her fiercely.

"*Major...*"

"*Lang, if you had any idea how much I want to put you over my knee and spank you right now, you'd be quiet and kiss me.*"

"But—"

"*Lang, shut it.*"

His hand slid down the door and cupped the back of her neck holding her exactly where he wanted her for his punishing kisses. His other hand started on her pants, pulling and ripping the fastenings when they wouldn't cooperate with him. As soon as he'd bared her sex, he lifted her and she wrapped her legs around his hips and moved until the thick rod of his cock was right where she wanted it.

"*Esca...*"

"*Don't ever freking walk away from me again.*" He wrenched open his pants and she gasped as the slick wet head of his shaft rubbed against her clit. "*If we have a problem, talk to me, freking scream at me, but don't walk away.*"

"*You just told me to shut the frek up.*"

He adjusted his grip on her ass and slid home, working his

length deeper with short jabs of his hips. She groaned as he filled her, her body not quite ready for him, but still desperate to take everything he had to give her.

He pumped his hips, each stroke long and deep as if he was determined to meld their bodies and minds into one unit. She took it all and lost herself in him, found herself in the fury of his climax along with hers.

His head dropped to her shoulder and he shuddered sending her off again. As quickly as she could, she disengaged herself and pushed him backward until his knees hit the bunk and he collapsed onto the covers. His arm caught her waist and brought her tumbling down on top of him. She didn't resist. Just lying with him and breathing him in was giving her life.

"Why did you go?"

His voice was low. She sighed and rubbed her cheek against his chest. "Because I couldn't see a future for us."

"You didn't give me a chance to offer you one."

"I didn't tell you everything about my parents. My mom was only sixteen when she met my dad. He didn't come to Etrusca very often. When she told him she was pregnant, she kind of assumed he'd be delighted, and want to make things more permanent with her."

"But he didn't?"

"He never came back." She came up on one elbow and looked into his eyes. "I don't want to be like her."

"What makes you think I'd do that to you?"

She forced herself to hold his indignant gaze. "Captain Trenx mentioned your mate is a very powerful senator on Pavlovan."

He half-smiled. "Yeah, he is."

"You admit you're mated to a *man*?"

"In Pavlovan culture we form mating groups of three, usually one male and two females, or one female and two males, or even three of the same sex." He watched her closely. "I think you're our First Female."

"Me? Hold on, I'm suddenly supposed to be in a *threesome?*"

This time his smile was more relaxed. "If that's what you want." His expression turned serious. "All I'm asking is for you to come back with me, meet Ash, and see how it goes."

She fell back down on the bed. "That's *all?*"

He was his turn to loom over her. His fingers became busy unbuttoning her uniform jacket. He threw it to the floor and started on her shirt.

"Just give me a chance."

She let him finish undressing her, and then watched as he stripped off his clothes to display the perfection of his body.

"You won't force me into making a decision?"

"No." He stroked his cock, which was already erect again.

"I'm only supposed to be on Pavlovan for a year."

"If you decide to stay, we'll make sure you can."

"What if I only like you and not this other man?"

"Ash?" He straddled her and bent to kiss her mouth. "Everyone likes Ash."

He pushed his knee between her thighs and settled himself over her, his cock throbbing between them. "Please."

She arched her back, bringing her already wet sex against the underside of his shaft and he groaned. "*Please.*"

"*All right.*"

He slid home and she wrapped her arms and legs around him and held on. She had a suspicion that it was going to be another bumpy ride.

6

———————

There was a reception committee at the spaceport.

For them. For *her*…

Soreya tugged nervously at the collar of her uniform and tried not to look at Esca. After three days in his bed, she missed being even a centimeter away from him. He stood with Trenx, just in front of her as the steps were lowered and they all moved forward.

A tall man with faded reddish hair stepped in front of them and smiled graciously. Was it Ash? Soreya felt no vibe off him, but Esca was definitely smiling at the guy.

"President Gowon. May I introduce Private Soreya Lang of Etrusca?"

She suddenly found herself in front of the dignitary and just remembered to salute. "Sir."

He took her hand between both of his. "Welcome, Private Lang. We hope you will enjoy your year on Pavlovan."

"Thank you for inviting me, sir."

"It was the least we could do after your act of courage in saving Major Esca."

65

Soreya allowed herself to smile. "I think we saved each other, sir."

He winked at her and introduced his deputy, his finance minister, the chancellor of the university system, and the head of the Pavlovan military who spoke to her at length about his interest in her abilities. By the time he'd moved on, most of the crew had dispersed leaving Esca, Trenx and her with the reception committee.

She turned to see Esca approaching a slim fair-haired male who had obviously just arrived. To her surprise, Esca went down on one knee and kissed the man's hand.

"First Male."

"Second."

In less than a moment, Esca was standing again and looking around.

"Private Lang? I'd like you to meet my First Male, Ash."

She found herself moving forward, her hand held out, her entire attention focused on the quiet face of the man in front of her. She wanted to touch him, to see if she could even attempt to understand the beautiful complexity of his shields, a protection system that rivaled her own.

"Private Lang."

His voice was as quiet and refined as she'd anticipated. He was nothing like Esca, and yet she could already see why they were paired. It was definitely a case of extreme opposites attracting, but where did that leave her?

"Senator."

She took his proffered hand and felt as if she'd received a static shock. A slight widening of his blue eyes made her think he'd felt something similar, but there was no break in his shields.

"Thank you for saving my mate's life."

"As I was just saying to your president. I think he saved mine as well."

"Then perhaps I should be doubly grateful." He turned to Esca. "Did you ask Private Lang if she is comfortable staying with us, or did you just assume she would be?"

"It's a separate suite. She can lock the door if she can't stand the sight of us." Esca scowled at his mate. "Shall we go?"

Ash turned back to Soreya. He was still holding her hand. "He's correct that it is a separate suite, but you will have to see us if you want to eat or leave the apartment. Would you prefer to be on your own?"

"I think I'd like the company—if you're okay with that." She added quickly. "I don't want to impose."

His smile was beautiful. "Don't worry about that. If it weren't for you Esca wouldn't have come back. Whatever happens, I'll always be grateful for his return."

Esca snorted. "He thought I was going to die."

"You nearly did." Soreya retorted, aware of Ash's amused glance on them. He walked toward the exit and she followed him, Esca on her other side into the V.I.P. area of the spaceport. Ash moved with the air of a man used to being waited on. He still made time to smile and thank the people who ran around him, finding his vehicle, checking paperwork and generally making their departure as smooth as possible.

The vehicle they were ushered into was large and comfortable. Esca sat beside her, one arm across the back of the seat and Ash opposite.

"I hope you'll both excuse me while I attend to some senate business." Ash said.

"He's always busy," Esca grumbled. "I have to make an appointment just to talk to him these days."

Ash ignored him, his fingers tapping over a communications tablet, his thoughts flying so fast that Soreya could hardly identify that he was transmitting information at all. And that was unusual. She was usually better than anyone she'd ever met. It was tempting to simply sit back and bask in his psychic aura—

the miniscule piece he let her access, anyway. His shields really were exceptional.

ESCA GLANCED from Ash to Soreya but he couldn't tell anything from their expressions. They both had an annoying ability to look calm and uninterested that he lacked. But he could still sense the tension in the air, the awareness that fizzed between the three of them like lightening.

He was damn sure that he was right and that she was their Female. All he had to do now was try not to frek things up. When the limo slowed, Ash caught his attention.

"Can you show Private Lang around? I've got to finish this call."

"Sure. By the way, her name's Soreya."

He stepped out of the opened limo door and reached inside to take Soreya's hand. Now she looked rather apprehensive as she stared up at the modern glass and metal building that housed Ash's penthouse.

"Here?"

"I know, it's hardly what we soldiers are used to, is it?"

Her smile was uncertain as she followed him into the private elevator. "Is Senator Ash not coming?"

Esca bit back his comment that if he had his way, Ash would be coming pretty damn soon and returned a more non-committal answer. "He'll be up in a minute."

The door to the penthouse opened to reveal Chase their housekeeper.

"Major! So good to see you back!"

"It appears that rumors of my death have been greatly exaggerated." Esca muttered. Chase looked politely blank, but Soreya choked back a laugh. "This is Private Lang. She's going to be staying with us for a while."

"Private Lang." Chase shook Soreya's hand. "It's great to

meet you. Let me show you to your suite." She glanced up at Esca. "Unless you want to do it?"

"How about we do it together?" Esca studied Soreya's face, and caught the edge of her exhaustion. "I think Private Lang needs her privacy and a good long nap." He smiled. "*Without me waking her up.*"

"*I don't mind.*"

He took her hand and led her into the three-roomed suite, which was identical to his own and to Ash's. "There's a sitting area and workspace, a bedroom and a decent sized fully-stocked bathroom. You should find everything here, but if in doubt, call me or Chase, and we'll get you what you need."

"Thank you." Soreya was staring at all the space. "Are you sure this is all for me?" She swallowed hard. "Since I was ten, I've never even had my own bedroom."

"Then enjoy it." Esca touched her shoulder and felt the tension running through her. "If you wake up and want company, come through into the central atrium. Chase will be there or later, you'll find me or Ash."

"Great."

He hesitated by the door of the bedroom. "*I need to check in with Ash. Are you okay with being left alone?*"

She smiled brightly at him. "*Of course. You go ahead. I'll see you later.*"

Frek, he hadn't thought about the ramifications of bed hopping. He'd have to talk to Ash who would be sure to know how to manage everything gracefully

Chase was busy checking the drapes were closed and turning down the bed. "Would you like something to eat before you take your nap, Private Lang?"

"No, I'm fine, thank you." She pushed her brown hair away from her forehead and straightened her spine. "I'll take a quick shower and then I'll go to bed."

"Thanks, Chase." Esca smiled at the housekeeper.

"You're welcome, Esca. I'll get your lunch after I've showed Private Lang how the shower works." She patted his ass. "Now get along with you."

"Soreya?"

"I'm fine, Esca—really. I'll see you later."

She didn't sound fine, and even he knew that when a female said 'fine' she rarely meant it. But he did need to see Ash…

"Okay."

Okay, he was a big fat coward. He escaped into the kitchen and noticed Ash's door was now open. Walking through, he caught sight of Ash stripping off his formal attire. He kept walking until he had his mate pinned against the wall and his mouth on his.

"I'm back."

"I noticed."

Esca reached between them and cupped Ash's already erect cock. *"And you're pleased to see me."*

"I'm always—" Ash groaned as Esca gripped him through his pants. *"Shouldn't you be resting?"*

"But I need this." Esca started on the buttons of Ash's fly. *"I need to be fucked hard."*

"Haven't you been fucked enough?"

Esca stared into Ash's blue eyes. *"No."*

His lover opened his mouth to argue, and Esca kissed him again. *"Fuck me."*

He turned around and headed for Ash's bed, shucking off his clothes as he went. Just as he reached the bed, Ash came up behind him and pushed him down on his stomach, his cock pressed against Esca's ass.

Esca groaned and arched his spine, felt the cold trickle of lube against his ass and the oiled flick of Ash's probing fingers.

"Yeah, now give me your dick."

He always forgot how big Ash was until that first push made him widen his stance and breathe out slowly. Gods he loved the way his mate stretched him, made himself fit, made Esca so horny he'd take everything the man wanted to give him. Ash wrapped a hand around Esca's cock and squeezed hard enough to make him yelp.

"You're sore. I hear you spent three days with Private Lang in your cabin." Ash pulled back and the slammed forward until he was deep inside again.

"That's right, I did." Ash didn't relinquish his hard grip on Esca's cock. Esca paused. *"Why? Are you jealous?"*

Ash went still and then started pounding into Esca's ass until he didn't have any words left to give him just moans and gasps and endurance as his body shook and shuddered with the onslaught of pleasure.

"Perhaps I'll make you as sore as she did. Take my belt to you." Ash bit Esca's neck hard enough to hurt. *"Make you unable to fuck anything, or sit down for a week."*

"Do it."

Esca started to come; his seed barely making it out between Ash's tightly clenched fingers covering his cock. Ash gathered himself and shoved deep one last time before climaxing in thick pulsing jerks. He rolled to one side, taking Esca with him.

When he finally pulled out, Esca winced.

"I'm sorry, that was inexcusable." Ash tentatively touched his shoulder. *"You're injured."*

"And I asked for it." Esca covered Ash's hand with his own. *"I wanted to get a reaction out of you."* He chuckled. *"It's good to see that you still care."*

"I love you. You know that." Ash hesitated. "If this is because of what happened before you left? I—"

"All forgiven. You were right. If Soreya hadn't been there I would've probably died."

Ash turned onto his back and stared up at the ceiling. "Do you really think she's the one? It seems so unlikely."

"Tell me about it. I couldn't believe it myself." Esca glanced at Ash's now serene face. "But you felt something, didn't you?"

"She is extraordinary."

Esca allowed himself a small self-congratulatory smile. "Her skill set is unlike any I've ever seen. She can plug into any power system and manipulate the information." He kissed Ash's shoulder. "And even better, she fucks like a dream."

"Esca…"

"You'll find that out for yourself." He sighed. "I wish you'd met her first. I think I've scared the hell out of her. She's never dealt with a male telepath before, let alone a blundering idiot like me."

"She must be in shock with all these changes."

"Yeah." Esca sat up and looked down at Ash. "I'm hoping you'll be able to help her with that."

"If she lets me. At the moment her shields are practically impenetrable."

There was a note of interest in Ash's voice that made Esca want to smile. His mate wasn't used to being shut out of anybody's mind.

"You're okay with me sleeping with her though, right?"

Ash's smile was wry. "As if I could stop you."

"And you're okay if she wants to watch us, or join in?"

"If that's what she wants, and if that's what the fates have decreed, who am I to argue?"

Esca leaned down and kissed Ash's mouth. "Imagine it, you and me and her…" He kissed his way down Ash's chest and licked at his nipple. "I think about it all the time."

Ash slid his hand around Esca's neck and brought him close. "Think about a shower and fucking me first."

"*That* will be my pleasure."

7

SOREYA CURLED UP ON THE COUCH AND TRIED TO WATCH THE still bewildering Pavlovan news. Esca had reluctantly gone to see the military physician leaving her alone for a few hours for the first time. She'd been in the apartment for almost three weeks now, had met her new work associates at the university, got to know the staff and her way around the kitchen, and barely seen Ash. When she did see him he was impeccably polite, his shields as high as hers, and his attempts to get to know her nonexistent.

She sighed. Not that she'd made any efforts in that direction herself. If she was honest he was something of a challenge. She didn't know enough about him yet to feel confident enough to initiate anything other than the occasional have a nice day. He intimidated her on so many levels. She suspected he thought she was a complete idiot.

As if on cue, the outside door to the apartment opened, and Ash came in, his steps slowing as he saw her sitting there. He wore another of his impeccable suits and his hair was tied back at the nape of his neck. He should've looked too pretty, but there was a distance about him that made his beauty inaccessible rather than approachable. She still couldn't get over how he and Esca were a couple…

"Private Lang."

Dammit, she had to stop being such a coward. She raised her chin, smiled into his beautiful blue eyes and got that shock of recognition that made her want to either throw herself at him, or run away very fast.

"You *can* call me Soreya."

"Thank you." His smile was charming. "That would be nice. Between you and Esca and your military ranks and last names, I feel I should be saluting all the time."

Another charming socially acceptable reply with nothing behind it. He turned toward his suite. "If you'll excuse me, I'll—"

She shot to her feet. "I feel like I'm making you uncomfortable in your own home. Do you want me to leave?"

He stopped and turned toward her, his expression mild. "Not at all. I apologize if I'd made you feel unwelcome. That's not been my intention at all."

She sighed. "Now I feel like an ungrateful rat."

He held the door to his suite open. "Why don't we continue this conversation while I change?"

Soreya stomped after him. His rooms were laid out in exactly the same way as hers and Esca's, although his bed was bigger. She couldn't help but stare at it, wondering what he and Esca got up to together on those crisp cotton sheets…

"I have a bigger bed because I'm First Male. *Technically*, I'm supposed to host all three mates in one space." He unbuttoned his jacket and laid it over a chair.

"First Male?" Dammit, sometimes despite her shields he seemed to read her mind as easily as Esca did. But then her face had probably given her away as well.

"It's how our culture differentiates between mating three-somes. Esca is designated Second Male."

"I bet he didn't like that."

His smile was the warmest she'd seen from him. "No he didn't. At eighteen he was very vocal about it too." He gestured at his pants. "Are you okay if I carry on changing?"

"Sure, go ahead. I'm military. I've seen it all before."

But that wasn't true. Her mouth dried as he pulled off his shirt to display his upper body and muscled arms. He wasn't as big as Esca, but he was stronger than he looked. She blinked as he pulled off his pants and underwear and walked into the bathroom giving her an outstanding view of his perfect ass and long silver hair that almost reached his buttocks.

"I'll just be a minute."

She sank down into the nearest chair, one that allowed her an eyeful of Ash stepping into the shower and slathering himself in soap. Her fingers itched to help out. She curled them into fists and eventually sat on them. The Pavlovans were having a terrible effect on her morals. She'd gone from enduring her solitary existence to fucking an empath and was now drooling over another.

Her mother would be proud…

True to his word, he wasn't long and soon returned, a towel wrapped low around his hips.

"Do you want to go out for dinner, or shall I cook you something?" He asked.

She was too busy watching drops of water roll down his chest and disappear into his towel to realize he'd asked her something until he repeated it.

Twice.

"Soreya?"

"You can cook?"

"I love to cook."

She stared at him. "Why are you suddenly being so nice?"

He sighed. "Because I thought it was time one of us made the effort, and it's easier for me."

"Why? Because with a word from you I could be on the next shuttle back to Etrusca, and certain death?"

His gaze sharpened. "Do you really think I could do that to a female with your extraordinary talents?"

She hunched a shoulder at him. "You think I'm an idiot."

"Why do you say that?" He took a silk dressing gown off the bed and put it on.

"Because compared to you I am an idiot."

"You have the potential to be one of the most powerful telepaths in the universe. You just need to believe it."

"Huh."

His grin surprised her. "You sound just like Esca."

"Soldiers don't deal with meershit well."

"It isn't meershit, and I'll explain why, as we eat." He held the door open for her and she went past him, aware of his scent and the damp ends of his hair. "Esca won't be back until later, and it's Chase's half day so we won't be disturbed."

SHE FASCINATED HIM. Beneath her average looks and well-toned soldier's body lurked the mind of a telepathic genius. Even though her shields were perfect, he could sense that behind them lay unlimited power and a potential that made him crave her like a drug. And it wasn't just about what she could for him politically if she truly was their third. She called to him at a visceral level. He wanted her naked, his cock buried deep in her. He wanted Esca with them too so that they could give her everything a female could ever want in bed, and then even more...

"What do you want me to do?"

He checked back his first salacious answer, which would have probably had her running out the door or assaulting him, and pointed at the refrigerator. "How about some wine? Do you like fish?"

"Sure."

He got her to sit up at the counter while he prepared the fish and sauce and poured them both a glass of wine. She watched his hands intently as he worked and kept up a steady stream of conversation that surprised him. Had she decided to give him a chance to get to know her? Did he want to? Something was drawing him toward her, and he didn't like it at all. He was usually the one in control, the one with the superlative powers that everyone else deferred to. But she could be so much more...

"Esca said your father wasn't Etruscan."

"No, he was a trader. My mother met him when she worked at the space dock." She shrugged. "She always told me she fell in love with him at first sight."

"Maybe they were fated to mate."

"Obviously not for life. The moment he heard she was pregnant, he disappeared and never came back."

"That's surprising. Usually, if a pair bonds that fast they *are* mated for life."

"Not in this case."

"I wonder who he was?" Ash swept the chopped vegetables into the pan and stirred in the wine.

"Why does it matter?"

"Because they produced you." He pointed his spatula at her. "A telepathic marvel."

"Or a genetic freak." She blushed and took a long slug of wine.

"Would you object if I tried to find out more about your father?"

She held up her glass in a mocking salute. "Go ahead."

"Thank you."

"Will it make me more acceptable to you?"

He turned down the fish and swung around to face her. "Do

you care if it does? You already have Esca."

"So do you."

"Does that bother you—that I fuck him?"

"How could it?" She opened her eyes wide at him. "He's only messing around with me. You're his mate."

"I don't think he's messing around." Ash put the fish on the warmed plates and brought it over to the table where he'd already placed a salad. "Come and eat."

He collected his own plate, the half-finished bottle of wine and sat opposite her. Her moan of appreciation as she sampled the fish did strange things to his stomach and made him want to lean across and kiss the shine of sauce from her lips.

"This is delicious."

"Thank you."

"You really are good at everything, aren't you?"

"Obviously not everything. I'm supposed to be this great diplomat and yet I can't string a coherent sentence together when I'm near you."

"You sound just fine to me." She carried on eating. "Your shields are almost as good as mine."

"Almost?"

She nodded. "Now that I'm sitting close to you, I can pick up a little more."

He instinctively checked his defenses, and felt the brush of her mind against his own. "And what does it tell you?"

"That I find you fascinating."

He smiled into her eyes. "The feeling is mutual."

"And it terrifies me."

"Why?"

"Because." She put down her fork and gestured at the space around them. "I don't belong here."

"It's just an apartment. Surely what's important is who lives in it."

"And that's you and Esca."

"And you."

"I'm just passing through. It's just so foreign to me."

"You're not enjoying your work at the university?"

"Being a test subject?" She shrugged. "It's interesting and I like the people I'm working with."

"But you still don't think you fit in."

"I'm Etruscan. I was brought up to believe I was scum and existed simply because I was of use to my government. Coming here where everyone is a telepath is literally mind blowing."

"Don't you find it freeing?"

"Yes, and that frightens me even more." She blinked at him. "I'd never met an adult male telepath before I joined Esca's Special Forces team."

"And then you had sex with him."

She groaned. "Yeah."

"And then he introduces you to me."

"*Yeah.*"

He picked up her plate and stood up. "Not all mated couples have sex with everyone within their group. We can just link minds and not bodies."

"Really?" She looked up at him. "I don't know if it's possible to separate the two. When Esca kissed me…"

His cock jumped at the unstoppable visceral image that passed between them. He carefully put the plates down on the counter and turned back to her. She'd risen to her feet and was regarding him warily.

"Why don't you kiss me, Soreya?"

"What?"

"Maybe you won't feel the same as you did for Esca, and we can just be friends."

"Is that what you want?"

"I want you to have *choices*. You've been denied that opportunity all your life. If you don't want me, then I'm okay with that."

Liar. His conscience whispered and he thrust the thought

away. He would give her space. It was the least he could do considering that he'd do anything to fuck her, own her, meld with her, anything at all. That wasn't like him. Perhaps he was saving himself as well.

She rubbed a hand over her mouth and approached him as warily as a hunted animal. "I'm not sure if this is a good idea."

"It's just a kiss."

"And what if I immediately want you? Does that mean that every time a Pavlovan telepath kisses me I want to fuck them?"

"You're afraid of that, aren't you?"

"That I'm so desperate to be with my own kind that I'll whore myself out to anyone? Yeah, that scares me."

"Did you fuck your way through Esca's team and Trenx's crew?"

"No, but none of them kissed me."

He leaned back against the counter and put his hands on the edge. "Kiss me. I won't even touch you."

She came even closer, her gaze fixed on his mouth. He held his breath as she went up on her toes and touched her lips to his...

Gods...

Her tongue flicked a shy line along the seam of his lips and he opened his mouth and let her in. He closed his eyes and gripped the counter in an effort not to bring his arms around her and press her against him from head to toe. She leaned closer, her breasts brushing his chest, his cock thickened and throbbed between them and he couldn't stop kissing her, would've killed anyone, even Esca, who tried to interrupt.

Eventually she pulled away, her breathing as ragged as his own, her pupils so dilated that there was almost no color left. Tentatively he reached for her with his mind.

"Soreya?"

She pushed at his chest. *"Dammit!"*

He made himself smile at her, his mask firmly back in place.

"See? That wasn't so bad, was it? We're not rolling around naked on the floor."

She turned and walked away from him. Her door slammed loud in the silence. It took everything he had not to storm after her and fuck her brains out. He concentrated on breathing, of *surviving* the onslaught of emotions he hadn't expected from such a simple kiss.

He didn't do emotions. He left that to Esca.

Who would be coming back soon, and was far too perceptive not to notice that something was up. Ash stacked the dishes in the sink, dressed as quickly as he could, and made his way out to the relative sanity of his office at the senate house.

Esca closed the front door and listened to the unusual quality of silence in the huge apartment. Chase was out for the night, but someone had cooked supper. Had Ash and Soreya finally got it together? He contemplated the closed doors and headed for Ash's. There was no one there and Esca frowned. His mate was supposed to be keeping an eye on Soreya.

He turned and walked across the apartment to Soreya's door and knocked, heard a faint response and went in. She was curled up on the couch and looked as if she'd been crying.

"What's up, Lang?"

He walked around and sat next to her.

"Nothing."

He raised his eyebrows at her. "Female answer one hundred and twenty ranks right up there along with 'fine'. What happened?"

"*Nothing.*"

He wrapped his hand around her ankle. "Did you fight with Ash?"

Her color rose. "Why would you think that? What did he say,

I'll—"

"He's gone out. I haven't heard a thing from him." Which in itself was unusual.

She buried her face in her hands. "Gods. I drove the poor man out of his own house. That's exactly what I didn't want."

"You're not making much sense here. No one drives Ash out of anything. What happened?"

"He cooked me dinner."

"It was so bad that you're crying?"

"No! He was charming and the food was excellent. I just..." she sighed. "I kissed him."

"And?"

"And I wanted to rip his clothes off."

"So?"

She finally looked at him. "That doesn't bother you?"

"Not at all." He looked down at his thickening cock. "In fact it makes me very happy."

"That I'm a telepath slut?"

"The fact that you're attracted to the two males in a triad usually means you're their female."

"So you say." She scowled at him. "It just seems like a damned coincidence that the only two males I kiss happen to be 'the ones.'"

"That's fate."

"That's *meershit*. How do I know that I'm not going to feel like that about every telepath I ever meet?"

"Kiss a few more?"

She threw a cushion at him and he ducked. "Okay it is unlikely but that's what's happened. Sometimes you just have to go along with what's fated." He eased closer and slid his hand up to her thigh. "So how come you and Ash aren't in bed together?"

She slapped his hand away. "Because, after I kissed him, he made some banal comment and let me walk away from him as if it had meant nothing."

Esca stared at her. "Ash did?"

"No, that must have been some other poor male I forced myself on, that's what I do you know, force myself on unsuspecting Pavlovan males because I'm so desperate to be fucked."

He crawled over her and pinned her down onto the couch.

"Did he make you wet?" She clamped her knees together but not fast enough leaving him free to inch his fingers closer to her mound. "Gods you're soaking."

"I'm—"

He kissed her filling her mouth with his tongue, thrusting and owning her in the same way he'd be fucking her as soon as he got his pants undone. She moaned as he pulled off her sensible underwear and slid two fingers inside her, his thumb on her clit. She came almost immediately. He had but a second to wonder whether her arousal was for him, or for Ash before she unfastened his pants and gripped his cock.

He surged forward into her palm; enjoying the friction, already wet himself.

"Let me inside you."

She sighed and let go of his dick. He rearranged them on the couch to his satisfaction, angling her leg high over the back of the sofa and pushed himself deep in one fluid motion. He growled as she started to come again, and kept coming as he pumped himself in and out.

"I wish Ash could see this." Esca groaned as her nails dug into his shirt. *"I wish he was behind me right now fucking me, as I'm fucking you."*

She climaxed again and he drove her through it, deliberately opening his mind both to her and to Ash, letting them experience his pleasure alongside him. Soreya gasped as Esca felt Ash's startled reaction before he pushed back and shut him down. His smile turned to a groan as he started to come hard and long, his rigid length buried as deep in Soreya as he could manage.

It took all his strength to peel himself off her and roll help-lessly onto the floor.

"Better now?"

She looked down at him but didn't speak

"You want him, Soreya, don't you?"

"That's irrelevant."

"He wants you. The fact that you've got him running scared is actually quite funny."

"Not to me."

"Because you think you've just got the hots for any Pavlovan male who kisses you."

She sat up and pushed her hair away from her face. "You are impossible."

He winked at her as she flounced off into her bedroom and slammed the door behind her. She was just as rattled as Ash. It kind of amused him to be the only one who knew how he felt for a change. He wanted them both, period. And he was going to succeed.

The sound of a door opening made him smile and get off the floor. He left his clothes where they were and strolled out into the central area to find Ash about to go into his own suite.

Esca sauntered toward him, his cock reviving as Ash inhaled the sharp scent of sex, of come, and of Soreya. He halted just out of reach and ran a lazy hand down his stomach to his cock and stroked it.

"If you fuck me now, you'll taste her, smell her on me."

Ash's expression hardened. "Why would you think I'd want to do that? You should go and shower."

Esca moved closer and cupped the bulge of Ash's cock. "You saw me. You wanted to be right where I was, your cock in my ass as I fucked her cunt."

"I—"

"You can't even lie about it, can you?"

Esca started unbuttoning Ash's shirt. His lover didn't say

anything, but he didn't stop him, which was enough encourage-ment for Esca. He undid Ash's belt and worked on his pants, falling to his knees to draw the garments down to the floor so Ash could step out of them. Ash's cock was too tantalizing to resist and he licked at it like an ice cream.

"You're wet too, just like she was. You two make my job so easy."

He slid his tongue into the slit of Ash's cock and smiled as his lover's hand fisted in his hair. With his soldier's sense for danger, he sensed a movement to his left and registered Soreya's door was now ajar. He didn't know if Ash had noticed, but he was going to give the female the show of her life.

<hr>

Soreya put her hand to her mouth and contemplated turning around to run back to the safety of her bedroom, but how could she turn away from this? A naked Esca on his knees in front of Ash, lapping at his cock. Ash's eyes closed as if he couldn't bear the pleasure. She stayed where she was, watching as Esca straightened and stripped Ash out of his shirt. Such different bodies, but both so in tune.

"Fuck me, Ash. Right here, by the window where anyone can see us."

Esca walked over to the window and braced his hands against the floor to ceiling window; his cock was so long that it almost touched the glass. Soreya shivered as he played with the crown drawing the gathering moisture onto his fingers. He'd given her the perfect view of his rear. He slid his hand lower, between the cheeks of his ass and played with his puckered hole, dipping his finger in and out.

Ash took a step toward him and then another and another, his breathing as harsh as Soreya's, his gaze fixed on what Esca was doing to himself.

"Fuck me."

"Not like that."

She almost jumped at Ash's low reply. He'd seemed as immobile as a statue, as caught up with the sight of Esca pleasuring himself as she was.

"Smelling of her?"

"No, raw."

"But that's what I want." Esca added a second wet finger and rocked himself back and forth, the tip of his cock catching the glass with each sway of his hips. Ash moved even closer.

Esca groaned and arched his back until his ass thrust against Ash's unmoving body. Ash's breath hissed out and he wrapped a hand around his shaft.

"I'm ready enough, I want to feel you."

Ash's cock was as wet as Esca's now and Soreya had a sudden image of her holding them both in her hands, making them come. Her nipples hardened and her hand crept between her legs where she was already sensitive from Esca's lovemaking.

"Do it, Ash. I know you want to. "

Gods, Soreya wanted to go over there and beg Ash to go ahead herself. Would he be able to resist such blatant provocation? She'd never seen two men together before and now she wanted to more than she wanted to breathe.

Ash made an odd sound and grabbed Esca's hips rubbing his cock back and forth between the other man's buttocks.

"You drive me insane."

"I know." Esca reached back and took Ash's hand. "Teach me a lesson. Make me cry out, make me beg."

"Gods…" Ash guided his cock toward Esca's ass and started to rock back and forth. "You're still too tight."

"Not if you want to be in me." Esca inhaled sharply. "God's, yes do it harder, make me feel every stroke."

Soreya's fingers slid uselessly through the thick wetness Esca had left behind and she almost cried out with need. Ash moved again, his ass flexing as he pushed himself deeper and deeper into his mate.

"Hands against the window." Ash commanded and Esca complied.

"That's…good, Ash, that's…"

Esca stopped talking as Ash thrust forward again and started a fast urgent rhythm that Soreya found herself replicating. She was aware of them both, Ash's thoughts so tangled with Esca's that for once, there was no way he could conceal anything from her. Lust and love and, Gods, she wanted to come…

Esca's whole body started to shake as Ash slammed into him, his muscles straining to maintain his position. Soreya wanted to crawl between his legs and take his cock into her mouth feel him come against her lips. She wasn't even aware she'd moved into the room and abandoned the doorframe. Wasn't aware until Ash looked at her in the reflection of the glass and smiled as he pressed forward one last time and started to climax, his gaze locked on hers as Esca followed, his come hitting the window rather than the back of Soreya's throat.

She covered her mouth with her hand and retreated to the relative safety of her own room.

ASH STAYED PUT until his breathing returned to normal and then carefully pulled out.

"You knew she was there, didn't you?"

Esca turned toward him. "Yeah, I was hoping she'd be brave enough to come and join in. She certainly thought about it."

"You're going too fast." Ash shoved his now disordered hair back behind his ear. "You shouldn't go around trying to manipulate people."

Esca's smile died. "Why not? You do it for a freking living. She's our mate."

"We don't know that yet."

"She's our *mate*."

Their eyes met and held. "Then at least give her the courtesy of some space to make up her own mind."

"Like you are?" Esca shoved past him. "If I wait for you to declare yourself she'll be back in Etrusca."

"And maybe that's what she wants."

Esca's eyebrows rose. "Because you're too scared to get involved with her?"

Ash moved toward his door, scooping up his clothes as he went. "Good night, Esca."

"Coward."

He wanted to turn back and plant his fist right in his lover's face but that wasn't his style. Esca was the only person in the universe who could make him contemplate physical violence.

"She's got it all wrong, Ash. She thinks she's going to fall into bed with every Pavlovan male who kisses her."

Ash paused, his palm flat on the door. "So what do you suggest?"

"We take her out and let her kiss a few?"

Never.

He didn't reply, just pushed open his door, went inside and took the longest shower of his life. By the time he emerged, the apartment was silent and his cock was sore from his constant handling. He kept seeing that image Esca had sent him of Soreya beneath him, her mouth open as she climaxed, the clenching of her inner core around Esca's driving cock.

He climbed wearily into bed. He couldn't stop thinking about her. Perhaps Esca was right. Maybe it was time for him to stop being a coward and help Soreya understand her choices. If she wouldn't accept help from him or Esca, perhaps he needed to find a more impartial observer.

8

"I'm so glad you could come out with us tonight." Dr. Mayek smiled at Soreya. "We've all been wondering how you've been getting on."

"Yeah, with those two *awesomely hot* men."

Soreya smiled at her research partner, Dr. Bev Crozen but she didn't say anything. She took refuge in her drink and checked out the bar her co-worker had insisted she come to after their shift was over. She felt conspicuous in her Etruscan uniform, but no one seemed to mind.

"So how is it?" Bev nudged Soreya.

"It's okay."

"Okay?" Bev snorted. "You're shacked up with two of the most beautiful men on the planet, and it's just *okay*?"

Dr. Mayek patted Bev's knee. "Maybe she doesn't want to talk about them."

"Why not? Gods, if I was sharing an apartment with those two, I'd be yelling it from the roof tops." She leaned in close. "Which one's better in bed? Which one's bigger?"

"Bev!" Dr. Mayek was bright red. "I'm sorry Soreya. She's so nosy."

"I understand." She smiled briefly. "Actually, they've both been very kind and patient with me."

"Which roughly translated means the three of you aren't in a relationship yet?"

"Not officially." Soreya sighed. "It's hard for me to get my head around all this openness about being a telepath, let alone the concept of having two lovers."

"I'm sure it is." Dr. Mayek nodded sympathetically. "It's good that they're giving you some space."

Soreya finished her drink and Bev immediately handed her another. Despite her outspokenness, Bev was not only a brilliant researcher, but also a good source of advice on all things Pavlovan. Soreya had already learned that she could ask her absolutely anything and she'd always get an honest answer.

"So who's the most difficult to live with?" Bev wasn't giving up.

"They're both very nice."

Bev made a face at Dr. Mayek. "She's obviously a born diplomat like Ash. No wonder they got paired up."

"How do you know?" Soreya blurted out. "How do you know you've found the right people?"

"That's a good question." Dr. Mayek crossed her legs and sat back. "Sometimes at their coming of age ceremony the Oracle at the temple tells a Pavlovan who one of their mates will be."

Soreya nodded. "That's how Esca found out about Ash."

"And I found out about Bev." Dr. Mayek blew a kiss at her mate. "We're still waiting for our third."

"But what if the Oracle, or one of the people involved is wrong?" Soreya persisted.

"The Oracle is never wrong and," Bev hesitated. "Usually when you meet a mate you just *know*."

"Just by looking at them?" Soreya gulped down the remainder of her fourth fruity drink and felt it settle in her stomach like a frothy bomb. She really should've eaten some-thing before she started drinking.

"No, it's usually when your minds click, or you touch them, or something more intimate."

"Like when Major Esca kissed me."

"That would do it." Bev stared at her. "Why, what's bugging you?"

"Because I don't know the rules." Soreya sighed. "I've only kissed two telepaths in my life."

"So?"

"And I've wanted to rip the clothes off both of them."

Bev glanced at Dr. Mayek. "We *are* talking about Senator Ash and Major Esca here, aren't we?"

She swallowed hard. "Yes, so what if after years of depriva-tion I'm just hyper-sensitive to being touched by a male telepath?"

"You think you'll want to jump the bones of any telepath who kisses you?"

"Maybe." Soreya stared down at the table.

"Maybe you need to try a little experiment. A selective study, you know, like we do at work when we're evaluating the extent of your abilities." Bev raised her eyebrows at Dr. Mayek. "We can help her with that, can't we May?"

"Bev—"

Ignoring her mate, Bev stood on her chair and turned toward the open area of the club where a few couples were now dancing. She cupped her hands around her mouth and shouted over the music.

"Hey! Who wants to kiss a genuine Etruscan war hero?"

Soreya groaned and wanted to slide down under the table. Dr. Mayek was no help, she was laughing like a drain. When she dared look up, a line of hopeful males was already forming.

Bev bowed to her. ""Here you go, Private Lang. Enjoy."

Soreya guessed her face was bright red. "I can't just 'kiss' them!"

"Why not? It's the quickest way to find out if you just lucked out and kissed the right men first." Her grin was infectious. "You'd better get on with it. Esca said he'd be by to pick you up soon."

Soreya took a deep breath and eyed the first man in the line who grinned encouragingly back at her.

"Hey, I saw you on the news. You really are a hero."

She stood up and walked over to him. "I'm an idiot, but would you mind doing me a favor, and letting me kiss you? I'm conducting a scientific experiment."

FROM HABIT, Esca paused at the door and scanned the crowds of people in the club. The music was loud, the chatting even louder, and there was some kind of disturbance over by the bar. His instincts kicked up as he recognized his mate right in the center of the maelstrom. He pushed his way through the crowd until someone had the temerity to bar his way.

"Buddy, if you want a kiss, get in line like the rest of us."

"What?" Esca snapped as he stared down at the male.

"The kissing experiment. The line starts here."

Esca looked ahead and saw Soreya standing at the head of a queue of males; Dr. Mayek was at her side, and Bev, who was *supposed* to be looking after his mate, was keeping the line in order. Soreya was smiling and talking to each man who approached her and then kissing them…

Esca growled low in his throat and the man stepped away from him. He tried to catch Soreya's eye, but Bev saw him first and waved before coming down the line.

"What the hell is going on?" Esca muttered.

"Ash asked us to talk to Soreya."

"This isn't *talking*."

"It's an experiment."

"Which wasn't quite what Ash intended."

"Ash is an idiot. This is far more pertinent to the problem."

"And if I don't like seeing other males kiss my mate?"

"Then stay in line and show her the difference." Bev winked at him. "I'll make sure you're last."

"Thanks for nothing."

Bev just laughed and sashayed away. He had to watch three more men touch his female before he was standing in front of her.

"Private Lang."

She blinked up at him. "Oh *frek*."

"May I help you with your experiment?"

He didn't wait for her to acquiesce, but yanked her into his arms and kissed her with everything he had. She moaned something unintelligible and wrapped herself around him. He was aware of shouts and cheers, but he didn't care, his focus on proving his point to the woman in his arms. He dragged her even closer so that she could feel every dangerous, possessive inch of him.

Eventually, he wrenched his mouth away and stared down at her. "Well, Lang?"

"I'd like to go home now."

"And why is that?"

She cupped his jaw. "Because I think I've come to a scientific conclusion."

He tightened his grip on her. "Good to know." He nodded at Bev and Dr. Mayek. "Good night ladies. I'm sure Ash will be in touch."

Without waiting for Soreya to offer her drinking companions, or her conquests more than a quick wave, Esca marched her out of the club and into Ash's waiting limo. As soon as the door shut, he picked her up and sat her on his lap.

"Don't do that again, Lang."

"What?"

"Like you don't know." He glowered at her. "Just don't do it, or I'll kiss your ass with the palm of my hand."

Her eyes narrowed. "It was a perfectly legitimate experiment."

He glared right back at her. "It freking was not."

She held his gaze and then slowly licked her lips. His hand clamped down on her ass and pulled her tight against the hard length of his dick.

"If you want to kiss something, Lang, I have plenty of options for you."

He nipped her lip and she shuddered and squirmed against him, which did nothing to ease his raging hard-on. Reaching between them, he undid her uniform pants and shoved his hand down inside her panties cupping her sex.

"You're wet."

"Kissing fifteen men will do that for a female."

He thrust two fingers inside her. "Liar, that was kissing me. I'm the only one who makes you wet."

She started to move against him, and he groaned and planted his thumb on her clit until she came around his fingers. His mouth clashed with hers, and she kissed him until he wanted to come in his pants like a kid. He realized the limo had stopped moving.

"*Wait*." He pulled away from her. "Let's take this inside."

He forced himself to rebutton her pants and lift her off him. She smoothed down her hair and opened the door leaving him to follow her out like a lovesick idiot, which was what he was. He wasn't ashamed of it. He kept his gaze on the sway of her ass as she walked in front of him.

She kept walking right into her suite and he followed her stripping off his clothes as he went. When she turned around, he was already naked, one hand wrapped around his cock. He smiled at her.

"Perhaps you'd like to start by kissing this?"

***

Soreya reread the note and then frowned at Chase. "Where's Esca?"

"He's out tonight, Private Lang."

She glanced at the shopping bags on her bed, and then at Ash's invitation. "He wants me to *dress up?*"

"It's an event at the Senate. Everyone will be dressed up." Chase smiled. "He asked me to get some clothes for you to choose from. I hope I picked something you'll like."

"That was very kind of you, but what if I don't want to go?"

"Then Ash will be all alone." Chase looked sad and cleared her throat. "He was very anxious that you should come. He wants to introduce you to everyone. He said to tell you that your appearance would benefit the research project at the university—funding and that kind of stuff, you know how it goes."

"All right." Soreya sighed. "I'll go. I owe him that at least."

"Great, I'll let him know, and I'll come and help you get ready, okay?" Chase winked. "I'm a dab hand with the eyeliner."

"You'll have to be. I don't dress up well."

Soreya unpacked the dresses from the bags and studied them carefully. They all looked expensive and shiny. Did Ash like his females to sparkle or was this Chase's taste? That surprised her. But then any woman on his arm would be competing with his beauty, so maybe she'd need the glitter after all.

Reluctantly, she picked up the dresses, took them through to the bathroom and started trying them on. To her surprise they all fit. She didn't have the confidence to wear a full-length gown, so she put those aside leaving her with three choices. The one she liked most, and she did like it despite all her inner qualms, was a light green sequined shift with a boat neck and long sleeves. The fact that it covered up most of her was an advantage.

"Are you going for the green one?" Chase came through into the bathroom bearing another huge shopping bag. "That was my favorite."

"Is it too short?"

"Not at all. My mom always said tits or legs, but never both, so you're good."

Soreya pivoted slowly in front of the mirror. "My mom would've loved this dress. My grandparents would hate it."

"They're in Etrusca, right? They'll never know." Chase eased Soreya into a chair and started fiddling with her hair. "It's super-short but we can still do something with it."

ASH PACED the foyer of the Senate building, his attention on the doors to the street where he hoped to see Soreya appear. Chase had called to let him know she was on her way, but there was still no sign of her.

"Senator Ash?"

He turned, his gaze on the beautiful woman in front of him. He blinked and looked again. She wore a shimmering green dress with long sleeves and a high neck. The dress barely covered her ass, and made her legs look endless.

"Private Lang?"

She pushed a strand of hair behind her ear. "Yeah. It's me. Do I look that different?" Her gaze drifted toward the door. "Should I go back and change?"

He instinctively reached for her hand. "No, don't, you look beautiful. It's just I've never seen you in a dress."

She made a face. "Neither has anyone else."

Retaining her hand, he turned toward the grand staircase. "Do you need to freshen up, or shall we go through to the main reception?"

"I'm fine." She squared her shoulders as if she was going into battle. "Let's do this."

Despite her nervousness, she was a pleasant companion, with an easy smile and a coherent reply to everyone he introduced her to. Only he knew she was more stressed than she looked. He kept his hand on her at all times, smoothing his thumb over hers, or touching the small of her back. Was she aware that he was showing everyone that she was his? Esca would've been more open about it, but for Ash this subtle need to touch her, to *own* her was as open a declaration to his peers as he'd ever made.

He brought her hand to his lips and kissed her fingers. *"You're doing fine. Relax."*

"Yeah, right." She was blushing, but she didn't attempt to release her hand.

"Would you like something to drink?"

"That would be good."

He steered her toward the refreshment room and stepped aside to allow a crowd of people to exit the room. Soreya moved back too, and his hand accidentally slid from her waist and cupped her ass. He registered her sharp intake of breath as his thumb slid beneath the hem of her dress and stroked the curve of her buttock. His cock hardened in an aching rush.

"Are you wearing panties?"

Still surrounded by the crush of people, neither of them moved forward.

"Of course I am. They're little tiny things. Chase said I had to wear them or I'd spoil the line of the dress—whatever that means."

Ash sent a prayer of thanks to his housekeeper. He couldn't resist moving his thumb over her creamy flesh once more. If he stroked higher, would she be wet for him? Would his fingers slide inside her with ease? Gods, he wanted to find out, to bend her over the nearest table and finger fuck her until she was begging for his cock…

"*Ash?*"

Her mind brushed his, and he started to move forward, aware of her heightened breathing, of the pulse that throbbed in her throat and the thump of his own heart. Was he seriously contemplating fucking a female in full view of his peers?

"Sorry, let's get you something to eat."

SOREYA ALLOWED Ash to find her a glass of wine and load up plates of food for them both. They found a secluded table and she took the seat in the furthest corner. She was too shocked and turned-on by the all too intimate glimpse into Ash's mind. Her, bent over while he played with her sex and finally fucked her until she was screaming his name…

"Are you all right?"

She looked at him; saw the sexual need he couldn't quite hide in his gaze, and slowly shook her head.

He frowned and took her hand. "What's wrong?"

"Nothing, I've just lost my appetite."

"We can't have that." He picked up a delicate piece of fish and held it to her lips. "Try this."

She opened her mouth and took the morsel in, her lips brushing the tips of his fingers. He jumped as though she'd sucked his cock and Gods; it felt almost as intimate, which was crazy. She licked his fingers clean and watched his blue eyes narrow. How invigorating was this? She had the most powerful man in the Senate wanting her.

His other hand left hers and slid along her thigh beneath her skirt. Now she was the one shivering as he plucked at the thin string of her lace panties as if gauging how easily he could tear it. Her nipples hardened, but at least he couldn't see that.

He removed his hand and drew in a deep unsteady breath. "Soreya..."

She rose to her feet and he instantly joined her. Her gaze dropped to the huge bulge of his cock.

"Do you think we should go?"

"If that's what you want."

He was calm again, but she knew it was a front, knew that he wanted her just as much as Esca did in his own quiet way.

"I'll call for the limo." He hesitated for a second. "I need to go back to my office. Do you want to come with me, or wait in the hall?"

"I'd love to see your office."

She knew what she was doing, but for once she didn't care. The need to have his hands on her was becoming all-consuming. She followed him up another flight of stairs and into his large corner office, which had a commanding view of the business section of the city. While he gathered up his work, she perched on the front of his desk and studied the city she'd just started to become familiar with. Unlike her home planet, there was a constant buzz of telepathic thought holding the citizens together. It made her feel part of something for the first time in her life.

Ash stacked his paperwork in a neat pile and put it on the corner of the desk.

"The limo should be ready soon."

She smiled at him, aware that by sitting on the desk, her skirt had practically disappeared up her ass and that he might even be able to see her panties.

"Thanks for a lovely evening. It was far less stressful than I thought it would be."

He moved closer, his gaze fixed on hers and planted his

palms on the desk on either side of her. "I'm glad you enjoyed it. May I kiss you?"

He didn't wait for an answer and brushed his mouth against hers. Again, her body roared to life and she kissed him back, only their mouths touching in an intimate duel that made all the hairs on her body stand upright. He leaned in closer, his body now between her legs and deepened the kiss.

She whimpered as he sank down to his knees and pushed her thighs wide, his fingers trailing over the soaking wet triangle of her panties easily finding her already needy clit. He licked the silk, his tongue gentle until she was angling her hips toward him, wanting more, *needing* more.

He slid one finger beneath the fabric and pushed it inside, his tongue swirling around her clit in a slow, sultry rhythm that made her want to pull his hair and demand more. She climaxed so fast she had to grab a fistful of his hair and hang on through the waves of pleasure. He added another finger, the push and pull of each thrust dragging against her sensitive flesh and making her come again.

"Senator Ash?"

She almost jumped off the desk as the eerie voice resonated throughout the room. Her companion stayed right where he was, his fingers still inside her, his harsh breath on her thigh.

"Yes?"

"Your vehicle is ready, sir."

"Thank you." He sighed, licked his fingers into his mouth, pushed her panties back into place and stood up. "We should go. We'll be blocking the exit."

Soreya stared at him. Wow, his shields had crashed back into place so fast she felt like she had slammed into a steel plate. Gods, it actually *hurt* to have her mind ripped away from his like that. Dammit. Had he even let her in at *all?* She remembered how it had felt when Esca had taken her body and her mind, the sense of being one…

Esca.

She slid off the desk and yanked down her skirt. "You're right, we should go." Hopefully she didn't look like she'd just come around Senator ice in his veins Ash's long fingers. What was *wrong* with her? Give her a pretty dress and she behaved like she believed in Happy Ever After like her mother? It obviously hadn't meant much to Ash if he could detach so quickly.

She marched ahead of him, but it made no difference. She was still intensely aware of every vibrant sexy inch of him. He was nothing like Esca at all. If Esca had touched her like that, he'd be fucking her now, and damn the limo. Not that Ash had said he wanted to fuck her... had he simply wanted to show her that he was more in control than his mate? That she would never be allowed to get close to him as Esca had?

Old hurt churned in her stomach and she fought back a sudden desire to cry. He followed her into the limo and she got an eyeful of his hard-on before he sat down opposite her. Dammit he did want her. Did he think he was too smart to give into his baser urges? Was he waiting to get home to Esca?

As soon as they moved off, Soreya fell to her knees and crawled toward Ash. His hands fisted at his sides as she approached him, but he didn't speak. She reached up and undid the top button of his pants, unzipped him and ran her tongue along the already wet silk of his underwear. Damn him and his control.

She sucked him into her mouth and he shuddered, one hand gripping her shoulder, the other buried in her hair. She licked and circled the crown of his cock and then pulled his boxers away to reveal the thick hot thrust of his shaft.

"Mmm..." Without waiting for permission, she took him deep, using the techniques she'd learned before she'd met Esca to drive Ash toward a hard, fast, unstoppable climax. His hips bucked and he started to rock into her. She kept her mind blank, gave him nothing except the physical pleasure even as she foolishly yearned for more.

He came in thick, pulsing waves down her throat and she swallowed every drop. When he'd finished, she sat back on her seat and deftly wiped her mouth with a handkerchief from her purse.

"You didn't have to do that."

She gave him her best flippant smile. "Neither did you. I was just reciprocating. It's only fair, right?"

He zipped up his pants. "You make it sound like nothing."

"What else was it supposed to be?" She shrugged. "You were right. We don't have to *complicate* it with all this mating crap if we don't want to."

He studied her for a long moment. "I've hurt your feelings."

"Not at all. " She met his gaze head on. "A good straightforward fuck never hurt anyone. Thanks for reminding me."

"That's not what I intended—I—"

"Oh look, we're here." Soreya bounced out of her seat and flung open the door before either the chauffeur or Ash could reach it. "Night, Ash, thanks for a great evening."

She rushed ahead of him before he saw her cry and reached the door of the apartment a good few seconds ahead of him. Unfortunately, she didn't have the correct access code. With a low sound she leaned her head against the door and breathed deeply. It seemed she was shut out of everything tonight.

"Soreya, will you just—."

"Open the damn door, will you?"

He complied, but he caught her elbow. "Wait."

"Why? You've proved you can shut me out far more effectively than I can you, so congratulations, you win at something. Now why don't you go and find Esca and fuck his brains out?"

His grip tightened, and he swung her around to face him.

"I wasn't trying to prove a point."

"You damn well were." She glared at him. "Let go of me, Ash."

"You don't understand."

"Let *go* of me."

He yanked her so close that his nose was an inch from hers and snarled. "I'll let go when you stop walking away from me as if I'm some sort of saint who doesn't have any feelings, who—" He swallowed hard and abruptly released her.

"That's why you don't like me." Soreya smiled at him. "Because I get under your skin." She kissed him on the mouth. "I much prefer to see you lose your temper than hide behind your shields and shut me out. What the hell are you afraid of anyway? I'm the one with everything to lose. Goodnight, Senator. Sleep well."

She left him standing in the kitchen and made sure to lock her door before she put herself to bed. At this point, she didn't even care if he liked her or not, or whether she liked him. She just couldn't stand for him to win. A reluctant smile curled her lips as she surveyed the wreck of her bathroom after the party preparations. Whatever Ash did with his anger and his fake indifference hopefully he'd learned not to lay them on her.

"WHY ARE you standing there staring into space?" Esca halted, and studied Ash who appeared to be rooted to the spot, his gaze fixed on Soreya's door. "Are you contemplating breaking her door down?"

Ash turned toward him. "I'm just trying to make sense of female logic."

"Ha! Did you have a good evening?"

"It depends how you define 'good'."

"Well you didn't end up in Soreya's bed."

Ash let out his breath. "Are you sure you want that to happen?"

"You and her? Gods, yes—as long as I'm invited along."

"She thinks I'm using her."

"And how did she come to that conclusion?"

"Because I kept her out of my thoughts when I…"

"When you what?"

Ash lowered his voice. "When I kissed her and finger fucked her in my office."

Esca's cock kicked up. "How was it?"

"Don't." Ash walked toward his suite. "Didn't you hear me? I tried to keep her out, I tried to control her with just the physical, and she didn't like it."

"The sex?"

The look Ash cast him was eloquently dismissive. "I shut her out. She retaliated by doing the same to me, and I lost my temper."

Esca paused at the door to gape at his First Male. "Wow, and I missed it."

Ash started to undress, his motions uncharacteristically jerky. "She kept walking away from me."

"She does have an annoying habit of doing that."

Ash pulled down his pants and Esca inhaled the unmistakable scent of sex and Soreya. "She touched you though, didn't she?" He advanced on his mate.

"Does that make you angry?"

"You're kidding, right?" He stroked Ash's cock. "The thought of my mouth on you after hers is so freking hot I might come in my pants." With a sigh he fell to his knees. "And while I'm sucking you off, you're going to tell me exactly what happened between you and Private Lang so that I can compare her version of events with yours in the morning."

9

SOREYA ATE ANOTHER MOUTHFUL OF EGGS AND STARED GLUMLY over the city. She'd grown to love the view and everything about the apartment.

"Morning, Lang."

She looked up and found Esca helping himself to Chase's idea of a quick breakfast, which was her idea of a feast. He wore a pair of running shorts low on his hips, his military tags and nothing else.

"What's up? You look like it's your birthday, and no one remembered."

She put down her fork. "I think I should find somewhere else to live."

"Why?" He set his plate on the countertop beside hers and sat down.

"Because Ash…" She couldn't even finish the sentence.

"Ash is an idiot."

"That's what Bev says." Soreya took a gulp of juice. "But he isn't, is he? He knows exactly what he wants, and that's you. I'm just in the way."

"That's not true. He's just not used to—"

"Being challenged?"

He shrugged. "I challenge him all the time. I drive him freking nuts, so it's not that."

"Then he just doesn't like me."

Esca chuckled. "Yeah, he finger fucks you at *work,* and he doesn't like you. He's never touched me in his office. He's all about the firm line between his public and private lives." He grinned. "Wanting you that much must have shocked the hell out of him. I just wish I'd been there." His smile faded. "Do you want him?"

"Would it be okay if I did?" He nodded and she nodded right back at him. "It's kind of frightening."

"I get that. I felt the same way about both of you."

"It's hard for me to ask for what I want." She confessed.

"Hard for Ash too. Sometimes I think I should get you both naked and lock you in a room together until you sort it out." His expression turned dreamy. "As long as I could watch what happened, of course."

"So you're saying I'll need to be brave if I want him."

"Yeah, you'll have to make him declare himself. He's mortified by how he behaved last night, and thinks you'll never speak to him again."

"I was glad he lost his temper. At least he wasn't hiding from me." Soreya squeezed Esca's fingers. "So you think there's hope?"

"Darlin' you just have to find a way to break down his barriers, and you'll never regret it." He leaned in and kissed her. "I've got to go back to base for a day or two, so have at him."

Soreya went to get dressed and called Bev to let her know she'd be late.

Her research partner's face appeared on the screen. "No worries, I haven't been to bed yet, I was thinking of taking the day off to sleep, so you can stay home if you like."

"Why were you up all night?"

Bev grinned. "Because I think I've finally isolated the telepathic signature you use to interfere with power systems."

"That's great!" She sighed. "I can go back to Etrusca now."

"You still want to go? What happened?"

Soreya put her head in her hands. "It's Ash."

"I bet he's running scared, isn't he?"

"That's what Esca thinks too."

"I've tested Ash, and he's one of the most powerful telepaths on Pavlovan. But you have abilities he doesn't have. Maybe he's feeling inadequate."

"That's stupid. He's…amazing. His mind is *beautiful*."

Bev made a kissy face. "So speaks his mate who isn't biased at all."

"Would it matter if I stayed here and just had a physical relationship with Esca?"

"You don't want Ash?"

"It's the other way round. He said we didn't have to have sex if I didn't want to."

"A threesome is strongest when all three members are functioning as a physical, emotional and psychic unit. By denying he wants you, he's denying himself the opportunity to take on your abilities." Bev shook her head. "The three of you could become the most powerful triad on the planet."

"Does he know that?"

"He should."

Soreya smiled. "Perhaps someone needs to remind him."

ASH STAYED out as late as he could, but eventually even the Senate building shut down for the night. Unless he wanted to crash at a friend's, or rent a hotel room, he had to go home. Even worse, Esca had checked in earlier to tell him he'd be away for a couple of nights. Perfect timing. If he didn't know his mate better he'd think he'd planned it. Hopefully he'd left it late enough that Soreya had gone to bed.

The apartment was in darkness and he let out his breath. Why would she want to talk to him anyway? He'd behaved like a fool.

Her door cracked out, spilling light over him, and he froze.

"Oh, it's you." She was wearing a tiny T-shirt that hugged her bra-less breasts and panties that barely covered her mound. "Don't mind me. I'm just getting a glass of water."

She was giving him the perfect out, but he found himself unable to walk away. She went past him to the refrigerator and filled her glass, giving him a fine view of her rounded ass.

"Soreya, I'm sorry."

She turned around to stare at him, one eyebrow raised, her shields keeping him out. "For what?"

"For manhandling you yesterday."

"Is that what you call oral sex on this planet now?"

He went over and took the glass of water out of her hand and set it down on the counter. "I liked my mouth on you."

"So did I."

He picked her up and sat her on the counter, placed his hands on either side of her caging her in and watched her nipples tighten. Her mouth drew his gaze and he leaned in and kissed her very gently.

"I'm a fool."

She placed a hand over his heart. "You're the smartest man I've ever met." She paused. "Have you thought about all the power you're denying yourself by not joining fully with me?"

He kissed her again. "Sure I've thought about it."

"And it's still not enough?"

"Soreya, I don't want to force you to make choices that benefit me, or Esca, or the Etruscans. You've spent your whole life being dictated to. Even when you met Esca you had little choice but to go along with what he wanted if you wanted to survive."

"Is that what he told you?"

"It's what he felt, that he had no time to explain anything to you, that he just had to claim you while he had the chance."

"I'm glad he did."

He searched her grey blue eyes and saw only a wistful need in them, which made his mating instincts rise to the fore. He forced them back down. He could be civilized. It was essential to maintain his façade.

"I just want you to decide what you want for yourself."

"Why is it so important to you?"

"Because I never had any choices either. I was singled out as exceptional at an early age and great things were demanded of me. I've spent my life living up to that image." *Had he ever put that thought into words before? He didn't even think he'd told Esca.*

She cupped his cheek. "What would you've done if you'd had a choice?"

"Explored the universe? Run wild and untethered by family expectations or demands for me to excel at *everything*?" He swallowed hard. "I don't know. I was the youngest ever male ever to be elected to the Senate, and that's been my life ever since."

"What about Esca?"

He smiled. "He's my rock. He hates all the political meershit and keeps me sane."

"He loves you."

"I know."

"He wants us all to be together."

"I know that too, but it has to be your decision."

She leaned back a little to study his face, her expression calm. "Are you afraid that if you gain more power your life will become so enmeshed with the Senate that you'll never get free?"

"With the addition of your abilities I could rule the Senate."

"Is that what you want?"

"I want you."

She sighed against his mouth. "So?"

"I want all of you."

She drew in an uneven breath, took his hand and placed it over her heart. "I'm afraid."

"That I'll hurt you?"

"Not physically." She glanced down at the bulge in his pants. "Although—"

"What?" He bit down gently on her lip, and she shivered.

"I'm afraid that if I let you in completely, I'll never be whole again, that if you change your mind and shut me out, I'll fall to pieces."

He held her gaze. "Don't you think I fear the same thing?"

"But you're so *strong*."

"Not when I'm with you." He slid his hand around the back of her neck. "With you I feel *vulnerable*." He forced a smile. "Even admitting that makes me break out in a sweat. I'm not allowed to be weak. I'm *Ash*."

"What if I promise never to tell anyone and treat you like a god in public?" She moved closer to the edge of the countertop, and put her hands on his hips drawing him between her legs and against her sex. "I've tried to tell myself that you're too big a risk, but I don't think I can live here without wanting all of you." She hesitated. "I want to be with you, and if you don't want that, I think I should go."

"*No*."

He kissed her hard, his tongue in her mouth, his hands roving her body so that he could feel every inch of her. She moaned into his mouth and kissed him back, her wet panties dragging against the fabric of his pants and the hard ridge of his cock. He picked her up and walked into his suite, kicked the door shut and laid her in the middle of his bed.

She made no move to leave as he stripped off his clothes and came down over her, his aching shaft trapped between them as he took off her T-shirt and buried his face between her breasts. Cupping one soft mound, he licked and sucked at her nipple until she was moving against him, her hand buried in his hair urging him on.

He couldn't stop now. Instinct and need won over caution and training. He wanted her and he wasn't going to stop until his cock was buried deep inside her and their minds were joined as fully as he could manage.

"Ash, please..."

One part of him wanted to take her fast and hard, the other to linger and savor every moment of this amazing longed-for encounter with his female.

"Ash." She pulled his now loosened hair and he rose over her, parting her knees with his thighs. "If you don't fuck me right now, I'm going to cry."

He stared down into her beautiful eyes. "Don't cry." and plunged his cock deep. She was wet for him, but it was still a tight fit. She lifted her hips to take more and he gave her everything he had, his body, his mind, and whether she wanted it or not, his lifelong loyalty. As she opened to him, her power spread through him like the roar of a tidal wave, igniting his nerve endings, making him thrust into her as though it were the end of the world, and that he could truly become part of her.

She climaxed, her internal muscles clenching his shaft and he kept pounding into her, finesse and technique forgotten just a basic need to satisfy his mate and make her scream his name as she came.

"Gods." He didn't want to stop, fought the gathering need to come for as long as he could, and then lost control, and sank deep into her, his seed filling her with hot sharp pulses that wouldn't end.

He didn't even have the energy to roll off her and just lay there, his face buried in the crook of her neck as he remembered how to breathe.

<hr>

SOREYA STARED up at the ceiling and tried to piece the scrambled parts of her head back together again. The expression *I'm going to fuck your brains out* had never meant anything before now. Even though Ash had climaxed she still felt him, his cock inside her and his mind…Gods, the *power*…

And he'd shared it with her, given her everything he was. She touched his now damp hair and he groaned and moved onto his back. She went with him, his cock still inside her and straddled his hips, flipping the light by the bed on so that she could see him better. He groaned again, but didn't complain, his gaze on hers, his expression more open than she'd ever seen it before. Did Esca see this man as well? If so, he'd given her a precious gift.

While he watched her, she traced a finger over the sharp edges of his cheekbones, his firm jaw and incredibly tough, sexy mouth. He touched the tip of his tongue to the tip of her finger and it felt like an electric shock.

"Mmm." He shuddered. Inside her his cock jerked.

She continued her exploration, running her hands over his shoulders and muscled arms, the soft fair hair on his chest and his tight nipples. Leaning forward she let him see her tongue flick them, felt him grow even larger. His hand moved to cup her ass pressing her against him, his fingers dipping between her buttocks to where they were still joined and wet. As he circled the pucker of her ass, an image seared through her from him of Esca behind her, his cock wet and ready to penetrate her. Her clit throbbed and she clenched her inner muscles around his thickening shaft.

"*Would you like that?*" His wet fingertip probed her and she shuddered. "*Esca and me?*"

"*I don't know.*"

"Liar." He smiled at her and rocked his hips until she caught her breath and started moving over him. *"You've thought about it."*

"How do you know?"

"I'm in your head, you can't hide your desires from me any longer. And that's how it is supposed to be. The three of us united in all ways." His finger slid deeper and she gasped. *"You watched us fuck. You liked that too."*

She rose over him and then slowly lowered herself down on his still thickening cock. *"I'd like to see you do it again."*

"I'd like that too, and this time, instead of running away, you can join in, suck cock, have one of us using their mouth on you until you come, or decide who you want to fuck."

She moved faster, one hand gripping his shoulder as she ground herself against him. He took her hand and placed it over her clit.

"Come for me."

She was so sensitive that it didn't take long for her to fall apart and sink into pure sensation. He wrapped a hand around her neck and brought her down to him, his hips thrusting, his mouth sucking at her nipple until she was mindless with the pleasure and only capable of powering her way to a climax using his body in anyway she needed it.

She hadn't believe her climax could be more intense than the first one they'd shared, but she wailed with the pleasure of it as he fucked her back, his feet flat on the bed, one arm keeping her rammed down on his incredible cock as she couldn't stop coming. He came and she felt every spasm and shiver of his heat and wetness and Gods, she wanted it again.

"Give me a few minutes," he murmured as if he'd caught her last thought.

Of course he had…She collapsed over him and listened to the erratic beat of his heart. She'd never be the same ever again. Hot tears crowded her throat and she let them fall, defenseless for the first time and not sure if she liked it.

"Soreya?"

"I'm fine."

He sighed, "If it's any consolation, I feel like joining you."

She raised her head an inch to look into his icy blue eyes. His smile was wry.

"I'm terrified. You are…" he shook his head. "So much more than I ever dreamed of. How can I ever live up to you, and give you what you need?"

She managed a watery smile. "I suppose we'll both have to try our bests."

He kissed her forehead. "After we sleep for a while. Will you stay?"

"I don't think I can move." She stroked his chest. "Not that I want to."

"In the olden days a mated couple met at the temple and stayed there for at least a week in bed with each other. I can understand why now. When Esca comes back, we'll have to take a few days off and just stay in bed."

"Mmm…" She yawned and cuddled against him.

He gathered her close. "Go to sleep. I promise I'll still be here when you wake up." He finished the thought in her head. *"There's nowhere else on this planet I'd rather be."*

10

"Ash is here to pick you up—again." Bev said with a lascivious wink and a stage whisper.

Soreya shut down her workstation and hoped she wasn't blushing too hard. Ever since that first night together they'd spent every moment they could having the most incredible sex. Even just thinking about him waiting for her made her wet.

She pushed in her chair. "I'll see you tomorrow then, Bev."

"If you can see and walk straight," Bev muttered.

Soreya pretended not to hear, and hurried out toward the front of the building where Ash's limo awaited her.

"Private Lang?"

"Yes?" She paused to look behind her.

"Are you meeting Senator Ash?"

"Yes I am."

He held out an envelope. "Can you give him this? It's the information he requested from the ancestral database."

"Sure." She took the envelope and stuffed it in her bag; her mind already too deeply connected with Ash's to pay attention to another person. Continuing down the steps, she spied the limo and headed straight for it. Ash was in full business mode and was engrossed in conversation. He smiled at her and she sat quietly waiting for him to finish. After a couple of minutes, she put her hand on his knee, and walked her fingers up his thigh toward his groin.

He didn't stop communicating, but he didn't stop her either. With a grin, she cupped his balls and rubbed her thumb slowly up and down the rapidly lengthening side of his cock. After another minute, his hand clamped down over hers and held her still. He was so aroused that she could feel the fast beat of his heart through his cock. Undeterred, she hooked her knee over his thigh and rubbed herself against the hard muscles of his leg until her panties were wet, and the scent of her arousal was all around them.

His expression tightened as his fingers slid into her from behind and pumped back and forth. She had to bite her lip to keep from moaning. It took her a minute to notice the limo had stopped moving. With a sigh, she disentangled herself from Ash, got out and walked to the elevator. He was slower, but she didn't wait for him. If he wanted her, he knew where to find her.

There was no sign of Chase, so Soreya headed straight for Ash's bedroom, stripped off her clothes and sat on the side of the enormous bed.

"Well that's a nice way to welcome a man home."

She jumped as Esca appeared at the bathroom door, his appreciative gaze roving over her nakedness. He'd obviously just come out of the shower and quickly discarded his towel. He came toward her and spread her knees wide, bending his head to kiss her already aroused clit and lick his way around her wet, swollen lips. She moaned and put her hand into his hair, her gaze locking with Ash's who had just come in to the suite.

His slow smile took her breath away as he advanced toward them.

"*Don't stop, Esca.*"

"I have no intention of stopping. I'm going to make her come and then it's your turn."

Soreya shivered at the rough note of command in Esca's voice and then forgot about anything except his mouth bringing her closer and closer to coming. Ash climbed onto the bed behind her, his hands on her breasts, his naked chest pressed to her back. He teased her nipples between his fingers and thumbs as Esca thrust his tongue inside her until she climaxed in huge shuddering waves.

When he raised his head, he grinned at her and stood up, his fingers replacing his mouth. "Ash, let me see that nice big cock of yours."

Ash moved to Soreya's side and Esca reached out his other hand and wrapped it around the base of Ash's cock. Keeping a steady rhythm he played with them both until Ash started to groan and thrust his hips into Esca's willing hand.

"Fuck her for me, Ash, let me see."

Esca gently pushed Soreya down onto her back. Ash was immediately over her, his cock filling her in one thrust. She cried out and wrapped her legs high around his hips.

"*Gods…*" Esca breathed. "*Let me fuck you while you fuck Soreya, Ash, let me in.*"

Ash didn't even have to ask her if it was okay, their three minds were flowing together, so smoothly and completely that communicating was as instinctive as breathing. They both knew she wanted them, that Esca would simply complete their triad and unite them.

Ash's breath hissed out as Esca pushed deep inside him, pushing him into Soreya, who watched both of them avidly. He had no will of his own, trapped between the two bodies of his demanding mates, fucking Soreya as Esca fucked him. For the first time in his adult life he simply gave into their control, allowed them both to use his body as he used theirs, and found a sense of place and satisfaction he'd never realized existed.

He wrenched his mouth away from Soreya's and kissed his way down to her breasts, thrusting his ass back at Esca, and allowing his Second the opportunity to lean around him and kiss their female. Pleasure exploded through him. He wasn't sure who was coming, only that he had to come too. Esca drew away from him and collapsed onto the sheets allowing Ash to move off Soreya.

She had a dazed look on her face that he suspected he shared. Esca loped an arm around his neck and kissed him.

"Let's shower. I want Soreya to be in the middle next time."

"Next time?" Soreya groaned. "*Both* of you?"

Esca's hand drifted lower to cup Ash's balls. "Unless you'd rather just watch Ash fuck me?"

Her eyes widened and Ash's cock kicked up making Esca laugh. He put his hand over Esca's.

"We can do both, you know, in stages, so let's shower anyway. Some of us have had a long day."

Esca's rubbed Soreya's hair with the towel and insisted on carrying her back to bed. Apparently, showering with two people who wanted to fuck you ended up with not a lot of washing, and rather a lot of foreplay, which was fine by him. He knelt on the bed facing Soreya and Ash climbed up beside him. She gave him an airy wave.

"Why don't you start without me?"

Esca grinned at her. "You just want to see me being fucked, don't you?"

"Consider me an admiring audience of one."

Ash kissed his shoulder. "The only audience we'll ever have. I'll fuck him from behind, Soreya, so that you get a good look at him, and can join in if you want to."

He knelt behind Esca, his chest to his mate's back and

brought his hands around He played with his lover's nipples until Esca groaned and thrust his ass back. Then Ash moved lower to toy with Esca's dick. Unlike Ash, Esca wasn't cut and he always enjoyed the way Ash slid his foreskin up and down over his wet crown, revealing his need and then hiding it again.

"Soreya, lick him. He wants you." Ash bit Esca's shoulder hard enough to make him jerk. *"Tell her."*

"Whatever Lang want to do is fine by me." Esca groaned.

Ash looked over at Soreya who was watching them, one hand buried between her thighs.

"What do you want to do?" He drew Esca's thick wet cock away from his stomach. *"Your choice."*

She looked rather seriously at them both and Esca tensed.

"What? We don't mind. We'll do anything you want."

She licked her lips as if already savoring a treat. "I'd like to suck both of your cocks."

"Gods, yes." Esca tried not to yell.

Behind him, Ash's cock throbbed even harder. Esca moved until Ash was alongside him. Soreya crawled toward them and his gut tightened in anticipation. She stopped just in front of them and knelt up. His breath caught as she reached forward and cupped his balls and Ash's in her hands, rolling them between her fingers, stroking and playing until he had to bite his lip to avoid coming all over her hand. And she hadn't even touched his dick yet...

"Mmm."

She bent her head and licked his shaft from root to tip and then did the same to Ash. She returned to him, lapping and licking at his flesh like she was enjoying her favorite ice cream or something. Beside him, Ash murmured something incomprehensible and interlaced his fingers with Esca's as if he needed some support. And then Lang sucked his cock into her mouth, and he realized that Ash was right. They both needed something to hang onto.

His thought patterns mirrored Ash's so exactly that he couldn't tell where one of them ended and the other began. The exquisite mouth of their female who was intent on pleasuring them both willingly trapped them. She urged them closer together, aligning their cocks and then took them both at the same time.

For a moment Esca thought his brain had shattered into a million pieces, but it was just the sheer, freking, unbelievable *pleasure* of it, as she sucked them both. He tightened his grip on Ash's hand, and hoped he didn't break anything. They climaxed simultaneously, their come overwhelming the confines of their mate's beautiful mouth and pouring out as she tried valiantly to swallow.

Without even discussing it, they had her on her back, his mouth on her cunt, Ash's fingers slipping through her wetness, his tongue thrusting inside her, Ash's thumb in her ass as she bucked and cried out. He slid one hand up to her breast and played with that too as Ash kissed her mouth. His cock was already recovering and wanting more.

"Both of us."

He sat with his back to the headboard and brought her down over his cock to face him. She was wet enough to take him easily and he continued to grow inside her. Ash played with her ass, his oiled fingers easing in and out of her until she climaxed around Esca's dick making him even harder and Ash's entry into her ass easier.

Gods he could feel Ash working his cock into her through the thin wall that separated him from her already full of his cock cunt. The push and pull stimulated him even more. It was difficult not to start thrusting, but he held still, his hands firm on his female's hips until Ash was as deep as he could go.

Soreya opened her eyes and stared into his. He'd never seen anything so beautiful as her face at that moment.

"This is...amazing."

He guessed none of them could form coherent sentences out loud anymore and, hell, they didn't have to. Sharing this moment as a telepathic threesome was all about the internal, about the connections and the bond that he never wanted to live without. She climaxed and Ash started to move and then he couldn't even form thoughts because sensation became everything. Lang was right, it *was* amazing and he'd crave this togetherness for the rest of his life.

She came again and Ash joined her. Esca held out for as long as he could from joining them just so he could marvel at their pleasure, but soon he was sucked down into the maelstrom. And then there was no more him, just them, and that was even better. Emotion clawed at his throat as his come jetted into her and for a terrifying moment he thought he was going to cry.

Gods help them if Soreya didn't want to stay with them forever. He wasn't sure if he and Ash would survive.

SOREYA LAY on her side and gazed at her two sleeping companions. Esca lay on his back with Ash draped over one side; one thigh hooked over his lover's hip, his blond hair a tangled mess against the pillows. Before she'd woken up, she'd been cuddled against Esca's other side,

Sex with two males—if they were your telepathic mates was extraordinary. She imagined the horrified expressions on her Etruscan grandparents faces if they could see her right now. She was even worse than her mother who'd only shacked up with one telepath. Could she summon up even a hint of shame? She stared up at the ceiling and tried. Nope. She deserved this. It just felt 'right'.

But there was the little matter of her return to Etrusca in less than a year... Would Ash and Esca want her to stay with them long term? She'd learned never to take anything for granted.

She was fairly certain that if Ash put his mind to it, he could have her made a Pavlovan citizen in a heartbeat. But did she want to go back home? She hadn't said a proper goodbye to her grandparents, who despite her mother's behavior had taken her in, and raised her to the best of their ability.

"*What's wrong?*"

Ash reached across Esca to touch her hip.

"*Nothing much, just thinking through some family issues.*"

"*Etruscan ones?*"

"*The only family I have.*"

"*Is there someone you need to contact there?*" He hesitated. "*I can probably arrange a planetary link for you.*"

"*My grandparents.*"

He came up on one elbow, his glorious hair falling over one shoulder. "*Do you miss them?*"

"*Not at all. But I owe them. My mother was publicly executed for encouraging my telepathic tendencies. Everyone told them to have me 'put down' too, but they refused. I'm not sure why, because they made me aware with every breath I took that I was a burden and an abomination.*"

"*And yet you want to contact them.*"

"*I don't expect anything back.*" She took a deep breath. "*I just want them to know I'm safe, and that I'm happy here among my own kind.*"

"*Then I will arrange the link for you.*"

"*Thank you, Ash.*"

He leaned over Esca and kissed her cheek and then her mouth. "*Don't cry.*"

"I'm not..."

He kissed her again and she forgot what she was about to say and simply kissed him back. His hand drifted down from her shoulder to her hip and the curve of her ass. She moved closer and his fingers slid between her buttocks to cup and play with her wet sex.

"Are you too sore?"

She considered that as he continued to touch her, his fingers gentle.

"No, I want you."

He smiled as he climbed over a still sleeping Esca. "Now you understand why I have the biggest bed."

He knelt between her thighs and bent his head to kiss her clit, his tongue swirling around her already aroused flesh and then probing inward until she shivered and moved against the sheets. With a soft sound, he rose over her and positioned his cock at her entrance. He took his time easing inside, his fingertip caressing her clit as he rocked forward, his gaze fixed on her, his thoughts aligned with every nuance of her pleasure.

She sighed as he was completely joined with her and framed his face with her hands. Sex with a telepath was nothing like sex with the grunts of the Pavlovan army.

"I should hope not."

He took it slowly so that they could both watch his cock enter her and withdraw, each stroke a thick intrusion and retreat that made her resonate with pleasure and need. And it wasn't just her need, Ash wasn't hiding from her anymore either.

"Why didn't you wake me up?"

Esca sat up and studied them both. Ash didn't look away from Soreya.

"We were busy."

"I can see that."

Soreya turned to look at him. "If you come closer, I'm sure we can find a way to make you feel good."

"What do you have in mind?" Esca knelt by her shoulder, one hand wrapped around the base of his cock keeping it away from his muscular abs.

"This."

With Ash's help she raised her head and sucked Esca's shaft

into her mouth. He groaned and planted his hand on the pillow, leaning into each pull, his hips undulating.

"Now me."

Soreya released his cock and Ash took over. She didn't think she'd ever tire of seeing him like that. His body aligned with hers, his mouth sucking gently at Esca's big cock. They traded places for a while, until Esca was fucking their mouths, his need apparent on his face as he groaned with each dragging motion of Ash's mouth over his flesh.

"Let me finish him, while I make you come too."

Soreya wasn't going to argue with that and lay back to watch. Not that she got more than a moment to do that before Ash began to increase his pace, fucking them both, bringing them to a climax at the same moment that made them all cry out with the completeness of it, with the rightness of being entwined both mentally and physically.

When she opened her eyes, Ash took one hand and Esca the other.

"We have something to ask you." She blinked at them. "We want you to stay on Pavlovan with us." Ash hesitated. "We want to make this union a formal one where we're blessed at the temple. We want to be your family."

Esca's thoughts flowed into her, of them all together, surrounded by kids, and friends and, Gods she wanted that, wanted it so much…

She started to cry. What the hell was *wrong* with her?

Ash squeezed her hand. "It's okay, we don't have to have an answer right now. Think about what you want, talk to your grandparents. We'll wait."

"It's not that." She hiccupped. "It's just that I've never been wanted before, never had anyone since my mom was alive, it's—"

Their arms came around her, wrapping her in love and warmth and she cried even harder, until her nose was running and she knew she'd look a fright. Not that they seemed to care as Esca found her a box of tissues and Ash held her in his lap and stroked her hair.

"I'll arrange that planetary link for you as soon as I can, Soreya." Ash kissed her cheek.

"Thank you."

"Do you want to go back to your own bed?"

"I'd rather stay here."

Esca lay down again. "So would I. I've got a week off, so I'm good."

"But what about the lab? I—"

"Ash will sort that out. He loves doing that shit." Esca drew her down to rest on his chest. "Go to sleep. There's nothing to worry about. One of us will always be here when you wake up."

11

Soreya smiled as she wandered into her suite and considered what she would wear to work. She hadn't been in for almost a week, but no one seemed to mind. She rolled up her Etruscan uniform, stuffed it in the back of the closet and picked something more casual. If she agreed to stay in Pavlovan, she'd never need to wear the blasted thing again.

She wanted to stay so badly. Picking up her backpack, she made her way into the kitchen and drank the fresh cup of coffee Chase handed her as she checked through the contents of her bag.

"Oh damn."

She pulled out the white envelope she'd meant to give to Ash days ago and stared at it. Both of the men had already left the apartment. Smoothing down the creased paper, she went back into Ash's suite to leave the message on his desk. As she put it down she noticed the flap was open and could easily read her name on the paper within.

"Ash, there's something I forgot to give you from the ancestral database people at the university. Shall I leave it on your desk?"

"Sure, but you can read it if you like. You have more right to the information than I do. It's about your father."

"Do you already know what it says?"

"No. If you want to wait until I get back this evening so that we can look at it together, that's fine."

She stared at the sheet of paper. *"It's okay, I'm a big girl. I can handle it"*

There was the tiniest of pauses. *"Let me know if I can help in any way then."*

"Will do."

Behind his calm acceptance she sensed he was worried about her, but, unlike Esca, he had the sense to try and keep that to himself and treat her like an adult who was capable of sorting out her own problems. She appreciated that.

She unfolded the single sheet of paper and read the contents.

"DNA analysis of the subject Lang Soreya indicates that she carries fifty percent Pavlovan genes from the Meljan family." She turned the note over, but there was no more information. "Well, that's not exactly helpful is it?"

"What isn't?"

She turned to see Chase coming through the door with a pile of fresh sheets in her arms.

"How would I find out where a particular Pavlovan family live?"

"If you didn't want to contact them telepathically? You could look them up on Pavlovnet."

Soreya picked up her backpack. "That's good to know, thanks Chase. I'll see you later, I've got to go to work."

"Don't be back too late, I'm cooking your favorite dinner."

Soreya grinned and waved goodbye. Chase always said that because she thought they all worked too hard and should come home more.

Because she was late, she missed the rush hour into the city and reached the university relatively quickly. Her partner was already busy, her gaze fixed on the screen, shoes discarded as she twirled in her chair.

"Good morning, Bev."

Soreya sat down and opened up her workstation. About five hundred messages filed past her gaze, and she groaned.

Bev snorted. "That's what happens when you take a week off for mind-blowing sex, Private Lang."

"How do you know what I did?"

"I just looked at you."

Soreya felt her cheeks heat. "I hope I didn't disrupt your work too much."

"I'm only kidding. I'm just so freking jealous." Bev sidled closer on her chair. "Was it really that good?"

"Yes."

"Are you going to stay in Pavlovan, then?"

"I haven't decided yet." Even as Bev's mouth opened, Soreya kept talking. "Do you know how to look up something on Pavlovnet?"

"Sure, it's easy. What are you trying to access?"

"The whereabouts of a particular family."

"Of course, you don't know much about anyone, do you?" Bev returned her attention to her screen and tapped at some keys. "Here you go, what's the name?"

"Meljan."

"Seriously?"

"Why, what's wrong with them?"

"Nothing that I know of, it's just that they're like Ash's lot. Very high up and generally a bunch of snobs."

"Oh, great."

"Come and take a look."

Soreya walked over and studied the list of names on the screen. There were two possibilities. What had her mother called her lover? She couldn't remember.

"How would I send these people a message?"

Bev scratched her cheek with one long red fingernail. "Privately or publicly?"

"Definitely privately."

"Hold on a min." Bev started typing and telepathically transmitting information at the same time. "They don't seem to want to be contactable. You're probably going to have to ask Ash to get you an invite. I bet he knows them."

"And what if I don't want to do that?"

"Then you could try their business office. It's about three blocks from here."

Soreya considered that option. If she went over there, she could at least see if she picked up anything telepathically from the people she met.

"Wait—I have an idea." Bev said. "One of their companies funds our research. How about I take you over there and introduce you?"

"You can do that?"

Bev fluttered her eyelashes at her. "Well, thanks to you, we did just have this massive breakthrough about how to train Pavlovan kids to interact with power sources. I was thinking about taking you out to meet some of our sponsors so that they'd keep financing us. It's usually a drag, but everyone's been asking who you are since Ash took you to the Senate event."

"If you get me in to see the Meljan family I'll smile and talk nicely to any sponsor you like."

Bev held out her hand. "Deal." Now let me contact these guys and see what I can set up."

As the elevator doors opened on the offices of the Meljan empire, Soreya fell in behind Bev and followed her to the reception desk. She'd spent most of the afternoon finding out as much as she could about the Meljans, which wasn't much.

Considering how open Pavlovan society was, they were either surprisingly discreet or great at controlling the information stream. She guessed the latter.

"Good afternoon."

The woman at the desk smiled brightly at Bev and Soreya. "You've come to see Meljan, senior?"

Bev nodded. "That's right."

"Then I'll show you in."

She rose, smoothing down her tight skirt and turned to the right into a short paneled hallway with three doors in it. Soreya's feet sunk into the soft beige carpet. The place reeked of money and privilege and something else…something familiar.

Her gaze fixed on the older woman rising to greet them at the large conference table and Soreya almost stopped walking. Luckily Bev kept moving and held out her hand.

"Thanks so much for agreeing to see us." She turned to Soreya. "This is Private Soreya Lang from the planet Etrusca."

The woman studied her for a long moment before holding out her hand. "I've heard about you. Welcome to Meljan Industries, Private Lang."

"Please call me Soreya, I'm currently on sabbatical from the military." Soreya tentatively shook hands, shutting down her shields as tightly as she could at the same time. "I've been seconded to work at the university here."

"So I've been told." The woman sat down and gestured for Soreya and Bev to do the same. "I understand that you have some quite extraordinary abilities."

"I'm not sure how extraordinary they are. On Etrusca telepaths are something of a rarity."

"Mainly because the government has them exterminated like pests." Meljan Senior's mouth tightened. "What an unenlightened society."

"You seem to know quite a lot about Etrusca." Soreya commented. "Most people have never heard of it."

"My family runs an export and import business. We travel to all corners of the Trios System and sometimes beyond." Meljan looked up as the door opened. "Ah, here come some refreshments." She turned to Bev. "And how is the research program going overall?"

Bev started talking, giving Soreya the chance to sit back and simply study the elderly woman opposite her. Were family members able to recognize other family members? She knew there was a special link between trios because Ash and Esca had told her about it. Shielding as best she could, she put the question to Ash.

"Do families have special links?"

"I have to wonder why you're asking me that, but, yes, they do."

"Oh, damn."

"Where are you?"

"At Meljan Industries meeting a woman I think might be my grandmother."

She took the cup of coffee Bev handed her. "Thank you."

"Are you enjoying your stay here, Soreya?"

She smiled at Meljan senior. "Very much so. It is remarkable to be surrounded by telepaths."

"You're living in Senator Ash's penthouse?"

"Yes, I met his Second Male on a military mission last month. It was due to his connection with the senator that I was allowed to travel to Pavlovan to aid research at the university."

"How interesting."

She smiled at Meljan. "I'm glad things worked out the way they did. It's been an amazing experience for me."

"And for us." Bev piped up. "We've learned techniques we didn't even know existed. Being able to manipulate power sources telepathically will give our population and our military a huge advantage in many situations."

Meljan nodded. "And in our industry such a skill would help with space travel, integrating our systems with new and emerging economies, and making sure we weren't being cheated." She nodded at Soreya. "I'm very glad you came to Pavlovan."

"Thank you." Soreya hesitated. "Are all your family involved in your business?"

"Yes, they are."

"My mother worked at the space port in Etrusca. I'm sure she mentioned dealing with some Pavlovans at one point. I wonder if she encountered any of your family?"

Meljan looked interested. "I can certainly look up the records and see whether we've had any direct contact with Etrusca over the past thirty years or so."

"I don't want to cause you any bother." Soreya hastened to add.

"It's no bother. I enjoy researching our family's past. Sometimes it's quite fascinating." Meljan paused. "Senator Ash is out at the reception desk asking for you, Private Lang. I hope nothing's wrong."

"Ash, what are you doing here?"

"I thought you might need backup."

So he was no better than Esca after all and far too keen to involve himself in her business.

He sighed, *"I'm sorry, Soreya, it's just that the Meljans aren't the easiest people to deal with. If it had been anyone else, I wouldn't be here. I'm worried about you."*

Soreya became aware that everyone was staring at her expectantly. She rose to her feet. "I do apologize. It's not like Senator Ash to demand my presence. If you don't mind, perhaps I'd better go and speak to him."

She excused herself and headed for the reception area. Ash was pacing the small space, his gaze distracted.

"What's up, Senator?"

He swung around to study her. "Is everything all right?"

"Yes, why shouldn't it be? Bev was just introducing me to

one of our projects sponsors. Is something wrong with Esca?" She held his gaze. *"I don't need this, Ash. I've got it."*

"You don't know what they're like."

"I'm a big girl."

"On a planet you've never visited before." He hesitated. *"Did you get a sense of something familiar from Meljan?"*

"Yes. It felt as if I already knew her."

"Then the DNA results are probably correct." He slowly exhaled. *"What do you want to do about it?"*

"You're asking me now?"

"I'm trying to. If it were up to me I'd have you out that door in a millisecond."

"Why?"

"Because sometimes it's better not to know about the past."

"You think she'll repudiate me?"

"She might."

"Do you think I care? I've never been wanted by anyone in my family except my mom. One more set of relatives who wish I didn't exist isn't going to destroy me, Ash."

He smiled slowly and kissed her hand. *"Then do you want me to come in with you, or not?"*

"When I do what?"

"Ask Meljan senior if she is your grandmother."

She stared at him for a long moment. *"I'd like you to be there."*

"Then I will be."

ASH OPENED the door into the conference room and ushered Soreya in before him. Turning on his most charming smile, he advanced toward Meljan senior.

"I must apologize for breaking up your meeting, Meljan. I had a piece of information for Soreya that was vital for this visit."

"*You* did?"

Ash nodded at Bev. "I wonder if I might prevail upon you to step into the reception area for a moment, Professor, while Private Lang discusses something of a rather personal nature with Meljan senior?"

Bev gave him her best daggers glare, but complied, her curious gaze moving between him and Soreya as he firmly shut the door behind her.

Meljan had reclaimed her seat. "What exactly do you have to say to me, Senator Ash?"

"It's not for me to say anything, I'm merely here as an observer and to offer my support to Private Lang." He gestured at Soreya. "Private Lang is the one with the questions."

"I see." Meljan redirected her stare at Soreya.

"I asked whether your family had any contacts with Etrusca, because I believe that one of your son's knew my mother."

"The female who worked at the space port."

"Yes. She claimed to have met my father there."

"And what exactly does that have to do with the Meljan Company? Do you think your father worked for us?"

"I think it's a little bit more direct than that." She handed Meljan the letter from the university. "According to this, half my DNA is from your family."

Silence filled the conference room. Ash braced himself as Meljan slowly read the letter and then handed it back to Soreya.

"And what exactly do you propose to do about that?"

"Nothing." Soreya shrugged. "If I stay here, I just wanted you to know that we might be related. Sometimes people dig these things up and use them against the families concerned."

"I thought your posting was for a year."

"It is, but I'd rather stay here. If I'm sent back to Etrusca I will be interrogated and then executed. Telepaths are not allowed to associate with other telepaths from off world. They'll consider me too great a risk."

Her matter-of-fact acceptance of her fate made Ash want to wrap her in his arms and kill every Etruscan who ever threatened her. Hell, with the increase in his powers he could do it too; he could kick them out of the alliance with Pavlovan so fast their teeth would rattle.

"Is that why you've apparently allied yourself with Senator Ash and his Second Male?"

"That's a bonus." Soreya hesitated. "I don't need anything from you except one small piece of information."

"And what might that be?"

"Some idea which member of the Meljan family *is* my father."

"And if I don't choose to share that information?"

"Then I'll accept your decision. If he's still alive there's always the possibility that I might meet him one day anyway." She glanced at Ash. "I'd probably pick up something from him, right?"

He nodded. "Yes." He rose to his feet. "Perhaps we should give Meljan senior the chance to think about this matter."

"Totally." Soreya stood up. "Thanks so much for seeing me. I apologize that you had to deal with a lot more than you bargained for."

Meljan didn't rise, but she nodded, her expression closed, her shields impenetrable. "Good afternoon, Senator Ash, Private Lang."

Soreya's shoulders slumped as they reached the reception area.

Ash patted her arm. "That went very well."

"You're kidding. She looked absolutely horrified." She sighed. "Well, at least I tried."

"Don't underestimate yourself. You did a fine job. She needs time to think about this, and she'll probably have to consult with the rest of the Meljan clan. I'm fairly certain she'll get back to you."

Bev rose from one of the low chairs. "Hey, you guys."

Ash walked over to her and took her hands in his. "Thank you for helping Soreya, Professor. I appreciate it."

A delicate pink color suffused. her cheeks. "Well, duh, it was nothing."

"It was remarkably kind of you." He looked deeply into her eyes. "I'm sure you'll understand if I ask you to keep this whole episode to yourself—for Soreya's sake?"

"Sure. I'm not a fool. I don't want this lot coming after me any time soon." Bev shuddered.

"Exactly." Ash released her hands and turned back to Soreya who was waiting for them by the door of the elevator. "Don't worry about Soreya. Esca and I will keep her safe."

"I know, otherwise I wouldn't be keeping my mouth shut."

Ash smiled down at his companion. "Smart *and* beautiful. I can't wait to see the male who makes up your trio."

"Neither can I." Bev winked at him before raising her voice. "Hey, Soreya, why don't you go home with Senator Ash? It's already way past lunch, so there's no point coming all the way back to the lab."

"Are you sure?" Soreya looked from Bev to him. "Ash hasn't been bullying you, has he?"

"Senator Ash?" Bev fluttered her eyelashes. "You'd better watch out, Soreya, he's a terrible flirt."

"Only when he wants something."

The elevator doors opened and they stepped inside. Ash instinctively moved closer to his mate. For the first time in his life he wished he'd gone along with the Senate's demand for him to employ a full-time bodyguard. Without Esca's reassuring presence on the other side of their mate, he felt a little vulnerable in Meljan territory.

"I'm a soldier, Ash. I can defend myself you know."

Damn, he'd forgotten how easily she could read him now.

"I'm not worried about you. Who's going to defend me in a Meljan ambush?"

She smiled up at him. *"Don't worry, I'll protect you."*

"I'm counting on it."

His driver opened the door into his vehicle and he made sure Bev and Soreya got in first. At least inside they were safer than out on the streets…

"Ash, what the hell's going on?"

Frek it. Now he'd alerted Esca to his unease. *"Are you home?"*

"I will be in about five minutes, why?"

"Just be there. We might have a situation."

"Do you want me to meet you in the lobby?"

"No, I think we'll be fine."

"Got it."

Thank the Gods for Esca's ability to not ask questions. They dropped Bev off close to the university and turned for home.

1 2

"So at the moment, we have no idea how the Meljan family will react."

Ash sat cross-legged on the bed dressed in his silk robe, his hair loose around his shoulders. Esca was opposite him listening intently. Soreya sat between them watching as Ash related the story of their meeting with Meljan senior.

Esca scowled at her. "You were stupid to go in there by yourself."

"I was *fine!*"

"They're a bunch of crooks and space pirates."

"Hardly that," Ash said mildly. "They've spent the last couple of generations legitimizing their businesses and cleaning up their act."

"Still," Esca continued.

"I knew you'd overreact, Esca. I'm not a baby, I've been in the military for ten years." Soreya tried to match Ash's tone but she'd never sound so calm in a millennia.

"I've got this." Esca looked over her head at Ash. "I'll apply for some leave, so I can be here full-time."

Soreya slapped his knee. "I'm quite *capable!*"

"But—"

She climbed off the bed. "I understand that you want to protect me, and all that, but I'm not your possession, and I don't appreciate being talked about as if I'm not here!" She went toward the door. "I'll be in my room. If you want to have a *reasonable* discussion about this, then come and find me."

<hr>

ESCA WINCED as the door slammed behind Soreya with a resounding crash.

Ash sighed. "Nice job at making her feel smothered, Second Male."

"You can shut the frek up." Esca glared at his mate. "You won't be looking so serene when they've abducted her and sold her into slavery."

"They won't." Ash reached over and stroked Esca's foot. "Just calm down for a moment."

He tried some deep breathing. "Frek it, Ash! I can't! We've just found her. If she gets hurt, I'll—"

"I understand, I feel the same way, but you've got to give her space. She isn't helpless. You of all people know that. She saved your life."

He thought about her hidden strength, the way she'd gotten them out of the security wing of the enemy compound…

"Then what are we going to do?"

Ash smiled at him. "We're going to do exactly what she said. Go and find her and have a reasonable discussion about what we can all do to ensure her safety."

"She's still blocking us."

"She's still mad."

He wanted to tear her door down, take her in his arms and

bring her right back into Ash's bed. No wonder she thought he was acting like an asshole.

He was.

"Perhaps we'd better let her cool off for a while."

"I'll go and knock on her door and see what the response is. If she doesn't want to see us, we can arrange to meet up with her tomorrow. It'll give us all time to think."

"You do that." Esca lay facedown on the bed and sighed as Ash slipped out of the room.

He was back within a minute. "She's not interested in seeing either of us tonight. She will talk to us tomorrow if you promise not to be an 'overbearing pig'. That last bit is a direct quote."

"Figures."

"I also reminded her that I've set up that planetary link so she can talk to her grandparents about her plans."

"Well at least that's some progress. Hopefully it means she's decided to stay."

"Because of the time difference, the link is early tomorrow morning. She should be finished by breakfast ,so we can talk to her then."

Ash took off his silk robe and stretched out beside Esca, one hand resting on the small of his back. He rubbed slow circles that helped ease the tension from Esca's shoulders.

"It's all right. This mating with a female is hard for both of us to get used to."

"You're better at it than I am."

"But you have the skills we need to keep her safe."

Esca rolled over onto his back and put Ash's hand on his cock. "It's much easier with another male." He rolled his hips as Ash played with his shaft. "I can't believe I ever wanted to have to deal with two females. One is quite enough."

Ash leaned over him, his blond hair tickling Esca's skin and gently kissed the crown of his cock. "That's good to know."

He pushed his hand into Ash's hair and wrapped it around his hand, trapping his mate close. "Suck me?"

"My pleasure," Ash breathed.

DESPITE HER EFFORTS TO block Ash and Esca from her mind, Soreya was well aware when they started to make love. Several hours later she woke up again turned onto her back and resolutely stared up at the ceiling. They didn't need her. They'd always have each other. She'd rather not have either of them if they couldn't respect her as an individual.

She groaned and covered her eyes. Damn it that was a lie, but it was one she might have to convince herself was true if she stood any chance of getting away from them. At least Ash was willing to compromise. Esca was another matter. If they were to stay together, she had to make a stand now; otherwise he'd never change. She wasn't prepared to have children with a man who would treat his sons differently to his daughters.

For all her faults, her mother had taught her how to be independent and how to protect herself. And she'd needed to know those things. Not every planet was as kind to telepaths as Pavlovan. She'd want her children to know the dangers of their abilities as well as the strengths. But she couldn't stand to be controlled again, to live her life as other's dictated, otherwise she might as well go back to Etrusca...

And now she was imagining having children with these males... Men she'd only known for a few weeks at most, but felt completely at one with. Gods, her life was becoming so complicated...

"Private Lang?"

She opened her eyes. *"Meljan senior?"*

"I've spoken to my sons. They would both like to meet you. Can you come by my office at ten?"

"*Yes.*"

"*Excellent. You might wonder why they both insist on attending, but according to my records they both spent time on Etrusca. I look forward to seeing you.*"

The connection shut off as abruptly as it had started leaving Soreya staring into nothing. Two brothers, and either one might be her father. She hadn't quite expected that, but at least they were willing to meet her. Would she know which one had sired her as soon as she met them? Would she finally have a blood connection with her father?

It was both an enticing and intimidating thought. Despite what she'd said to Ash, being rejected in person would hurt. Unless she had her own children she'd never experience that unique connection between a parent and child again.

She checked the time and realized she might as well get up. The slot for the planetary link with her grandparents was fast approaching, and she needed to prepare for that mentally and emotionally. If she did stay on Pavlovan she suspected it would be the last time she'd ever hear or see them. It would be kinder to let them go and live out the rest of their lives without the stigma of being related to a freak like her. But she at least owed them her thanks for allowing her to survive.

After she'd showered and dressed, she checked her desk and saw the handwritten note of instructions on how to activate the link Ash had thoughtfully stuck on the screen. She turned on the screen with a quick mental flick of her power and implemented the security codes. She ended up on a page displaying the Etruscan flag and a countdown timer in the corner.

After a deep breath, she composed her features as her grandparent's faces swam into view. They looked so damned uncomfortable and so old that it gave her a jolt.

She nodded respectfully. "Grandfather and Grandmother Lang. I appreciate you agreeing to participate in this link."

Her grandfather nodded in return. "We weren't given a

choice. We are good citizens who do what our government requires of us."

"Still, it is good to see your faces." She tried a smile but it wasn't returned. "I simply wished to let you know that I survived the journey to Pavlovan and that I'm enjoying working at the university passing on my skill set to the next generation."

Her grandmother's mouth tightened. "So we've heard. How *could* you, Soreya?"

"I'm just doing as my government ordered and being a good citizen." She paused. She might as well get it over with. "I'm sure you'll also be pleased to hear that I've met some nice telepathic males." Their expressions became even more horrified if that was possible. "They've asked me to stay on Pavlovan with them and I'll probably do that."

"Did you say *males*?" Her grandfather demanded.

"Yes. There are two of them. One of them is a major in the army, and the other a senator."

Her grandmother darted a look to one side and then leaned in close to the screen "How *dare* you disgrace us like this? You're worse than your mother! And after all we've done for you!"

"I appreciate everything you've done for me." Soreya said firmly. "As it appears that I won't be coming back. I just wanted to thank you for everything and say goodbye."

"I knew we should've put her down." Her grandfather turned to his wife as if Soreya wasn't even there. "She's a slut just like her mother."

"Excuse me, I'm not—"

"At least she won't be able to spawn any more defective brats, we at least made sure of that."

She spoke over her grandfather. "What did you say?"

His smile made her feel sick. "We might not have euthanized you, but we made sure they sterilized you before we took you back."

Her fingernails bit into her palms. "Are you saying I can't have children?"

"Thank the Gods, no. At least we'll be spared that shame again."

She blinked once, cutting off the link and sat there in the silence. So much for Esca's imagining their kids, and of her hoping to have her own family. Gods, she really was an abomination. Her males deserved offspring. They at least deserved to know ahead of time that she was incapable of providing them before they committed themselves to her.

Tears plopped onto her desk and she realized she was crying. With shaking hands, she pulled on an extra sweatshirt and headed for the door. She needed to be by herself for a while to come to terms with what had happened and before she had to meet up with the Meljans who would probably reject her too.

"SHE'S NOT THERE." Ash came back into the kitchen. "And she's still blocking us."

Esca stood up, his coffee cup in his hand. "Did she leave last night, or this morning?"

"I don't know. I'll check her last log-in time on her screen." He went back into Soreya's quiet bedroom and over to her desk. "She must've activated the link because she threw away my instructions."

"What the hell did her grandparents *say* to her?" Esca scowled at the screen. "Can we access the link?"

"I doubt it. The Etruscans were extremely reluctant to provide one in the first place." He tried though; using the parameters he'd left for Soreya and got white space. "Dammit, why didn't I get up and sit with her?"

"Because she didn't want our company, remember?" Esca

slammed his cup down on the desk. "I hope she hasn't gone all noble on us again, and decided to go back to Etrusca."

Ash stared at him. "She wouldn't."

"Then where else would she go?"

"The university?"

"Contact Bev, she'll know if Soreya's there."

"Bev?"

"Senator."

"Is Soreya at work?"

"She was in earlier, but she said she had to pop out for a bit."

"Did she seem okay?"

"No, actually, she didn't. She looked like she'd been crying. I figured you guys might have had a fight, so I didn't get all in her face about it."

"If she comes back, will you let me know?"

"Sure. It must've been one hell of a fight if she's still blocking you both."

"You have no idea. Thanks, Bev."

Ash turned to Esca. "You got all that?"

"Yeah, now Bev thinks we're both callous bastards, and we still don't know where Soreya is."

Ash let out a long slow breath. "Perhaps we're looking at this the wrong way. How about we have faith that she'll contact us when she's ready?"

"This ties in with all that crap you were spouting last night about giving her space, and not overprotecting her, right?"

"Yes. If she doesn't want to commit to us, I'm not going to force her—how about you?"

Esca stalked back out into the kitchen and sat down at the table. "You'd better put on a fresh pot of coffee. It's going to be a long day."

Soreya knew from the dubious looks the receptionist was giving her that she probably wasn't looking her best. She'd tried to freshen up before she'd left the university, but the results were certainly underwhelming. She reminded herself that it wasn't a beauty contest. It was simply an opportunity to meet the man who had fathered her, say hi, and walk away.

She was taken to the same conference room as the day before, and stopped short as she got her first good look at the two men who flanked Meljan senior.

"Wow, you're identical twins." She hadn't meant to speak first, but it was something of a surprise.

"Good morning, Soreya."

She belatedly turned to Meljan and smiled. "Good morning. Thank you so much for facilitating this meeting."

The male on the left of Meljan stepped forward. He wore a black shirt with the company logo on it.

"I'm Dahl, and this is my twin brother, Teg."

Teg wore the blue version of the company shirt and remained seated. From what Soreya could see he appeared to be in some kind of wheelchair.

"Hi." Soreya shook both their hands and got exactly the same zing from both of them. Perhaps this was going to be more complicated than she'd imagined. She took the seat directly opposite Meljan and looked inquiringly at her.

Meljan waved a hand. "Go ahead. Ask any questions you like."

Soreya took the only picture she'd managed to save of her mother from her pocket. "This is my mother, Aria. She worked at the spaceport on Etrusca. Seeing as half my DNA is Meljan, I have to believe that one of you is my father."

The twins exchanged glances.

"We remember her."

"You *both* met her?"

Teg looked at his brother. "It's a little complicated. When we were young, we used to change identities quite often. Your mother might have thought she'd only met one of us, but in fact, she met us both."

"And *slept* with you both?"

"Yes."

"Wow, what a sleazy thing to do." She half rose. "I don't think I want to know which one of you actually *did* the deed now. Do you know what happened to my mother because she got pregnant?"

"No." Teg said softly.

"She gave birth to a child who was telepathic, which on Etrusca is equivalent to giving birth to an abomination. And *because* she kept me, and tried to help me learn what being a telepath meant, she was publicly executed when I was ten." Her voice was trembling so hard she could hardly continue. "And you two thought it would be *amusing* to fuck her and leave her."

Teg's face was ashen. "No, you don't understand. "I loved her. When she told me she was pregnant, I was *thrilled*, but I couldn't get back to her—" His face crumpled. "I had no idea…"

Meljan's voice rose over her son's. "Soreya, please sit down a moment and let me explain exactly what happened. Teg fell in love with your mother. He was too scared to tell me, and too scared to sign on for all the already infrequent Etruscan flights in case I noticed, and asked why he wanted to be on that particular planet so badly. Dahl knew about your mother and offered to help out when he was scheduled to visit. From what I understand now, they both fell in love with her and were hoping to bring her back to Pavlovan as their female."

"So what happened?"

"Our ships were refused admittance to land on the planet." Dahl spoke up. "No reason was given. We were frantic, Teg especially. We even tried to get down to the planet surface illegally." He touched his brother lightly on the shoulder. "Teg was caught by the military and beaten so severely he barely survived."

"They use telepaths in the military. It's the only option open to us." Soreya whispered. It hurt to look at the two men. Teg was crying now, and his brother looked equally distressed.

"We know that we have deeply wronged your mother and you, our offspring. We would be willing to do anything in our power to make it right for you." Dahl swallowed hard. "But we also understand if you never wish to see us again. We will respect your wishes."

Soreya looked at Meljan who nodded.

"I had no idea about this. I wonder whether the authorities knew about your mother's pregnancy and banned our vessels because of it or whether it was simply appalling timing. Etrusca always hated dealing with Telepaths."

She took Teg's hand and squeezed it." I've always been puzzled by the fact that neither of them found a mate. I didn't know that they'd found her—together."

Soreya got up and inclined her head. "Thank you for seeing me. I hope it's okay if I don't give you my answer right away? I need to think about a lot of things at the moment."

"We understand. And, as the head of the Meljan clan I wish to offer you my support, and the support and resources of our entire family whenever you need them—whether you acknowledge us as kin or not."

"Thank you." Soreya left as fast as she could and came out onto the sidewalk. For a second she simply stood there and looked at the vehicles rushing by, the stream of people, and the comforting hum of telepathic thought all around her. She loved that sense of being a part of something. Did she belong here? Did she belong *anywhere*?

It was time to find out.

She squared her shoulders and went down to catch the

public transit bus that would take her closest to Ash and Esca's home.

SHE OPENED the door and stepped inside, only to find both men sitting on the couch their gazes already riveted on her. Their hastily concealed anxiety reminded her a little of the Meljan twins.

"Soreya." Ash came forward. "Can I get you something to drink?"

She nodded, aware for the first time that she hadn't eaten since the night before. Stripping off Esca's old sweatshirt, she dropped it onto the floor and went to sit cross-legged on the couch opposite him.

He nodded at her before getting to his feet. "Lang, I'll get you a sandwich."

She waited for him to start yelling, but he busied himself at the refrigerator talking about everyday stuff to Ash as if it was a normal day and they'd all just come in from work. But it wasn't normal. It might never be that way again.

The sandwich was excellent. Ash refilled her drink while Esca cleaned up the kitchen and made more coffee. Could she just crawl into bed and face everything tomorrow? She sensed that if she suggested it, neither Ash not Esca would push the issue. It was almost amusing to see how hard Esca was biting his tongue not to say anything. But it meant a lot to her.

Eventually, she finished eating, everything was cleared up, and they all sat on the couches together. She took a deep breath.

"I went to see the Meljans this morning."

Ash looked mildly interested. "How did it go?"

"Not quite as I expected. I still don't know who my father is. The two males are identical twins. Apparently they were both in love with my mother, which didn't stop them pretending to be one person."

Ash opened his mouth and then slowly shut it again.

"They wanted to bring her back here, but Etrusca denied them planetary access, and my mother and I were stranded there for good." She pressed on. "They want to acknowledge me as their daughter. I told them I'd have to think about it."

"Makes sense," Esca said gruffly.

She gripped her hands together in her lap. "And then there was the link with my grandparents. I thanked them for looking after me, and told them I wouldn't be coming back." Ash raised his head, his expression alert. "I also told them that I'd met two amazing telepathic males. That went down like a lead balloon, and they told me I was a disgrace, an abomination and that by the way, they were glad they'd had me sterilized so I could just be a slut, as opposed to a *pregnant slut* like my mother."

Silence.

She took a deep breath. "So, here's where I'm at. I won't go back to Etrusca, I can make my peace with the Meljan clan and live with them, or I can stay here with you guys if you don't mind about the sterilized bit."

They moved toward her as one. Esca sat her sideways on his lap, her legs across Ash. Their arms came around her and she rested her head against Esca's shoulder.

"We want *you*." Ash murmured and leaned in to kiss her cheek. "If we want a family, we can certainly try for one, and if it doesn't work out, then we'll make our own. I bet there are dozens of Etruscan telepathic kids who'd like a home."

Esca lifted her chin and kissed her. "Ash is right. We need you more than the Meljans, and definitely more than those freking bastard Etruscans. You really don't have any choice at all."

Ash glared at him and he raised his hands. "Unless you want to have one, okay? I'm trying here, I really am."

"Oh, *Esca*."

Soreya found herself smiling through her tears as the kisses came more frequently, and soon they were a tangle of naked limbs entwined on the couch, their minds enmeshed as Esca sank into her needy sex and Ash's cock filled her ass. There was nothing but her two males, and soon there wasn't even that as the power of the triad transformed them into one.

One power, one being, one love.

A force she willingly gave herself up to for the rest of her natural life.

The End

Dear Reader,

Welcome to the Triad series, which deals with far off planets, telepathic humans, aliens and the occasional four thousand year old frozen Viking... If you like your romance super sexy and involving M/M/F bonded Triads then these books might just be for you.

I hope you enjoyed *The Power of Three*! If you did, please consider leaving a review at your favorite retailer.

If you want to read more of my books, please check out my website and consider joining my newsletter for the fastest updates and early contests to win new books.

katepearce.com/newsletter

Thank you for reading!
Kate Pearce

Chapter One

Arctic Region: 229990
Nimbus Science Station. Earth.

"So, how can I help you, Doctor?"

Neeve stood to attention in front of the new base commander who sat behind his desk, his hands folded in front of him, his rather harsh face devoid of expression. Captain McNeill was a lot younger than the last man who'd held the job, and a lot harder to please. Since his arrival three months previously, he'd set the base on its ear reviewing everything from security details to the catering and lab schedules. No one had a good word to say about him, especially the scientists who hated having their little worlds disturbed.

"I wonder if you've had a chance to review my personal file, yet, sir?"

He raised one dark eyebrow. "I can't say that I have. There have been more pressing things to deal with than delving into the personal business of my subordinates." He glanced down at his tablet. "I do note, however, that you are a Pavlovan, and that you have been here for almost three years. What else do you think it is imperative for me to know?"

Her cheeks heated at his dry tone. Part of her wanted to walk away, but she didn't have that option.

"Pavlovan culture is based around the power of the number three."

He nodded. "So I understand."

"When I arrived here, my posting was for three Earth years, which will end shortly. I was originally sent here with my Second Male, but—"

"Hold up. Explain *second male*."

"As I said, our culture is based on the power of three. He was my mate."

"Why not first mate?"

"Because that was the designation he received when he visited the Oracle."

He looked at her as if he expected more information, but she remained resolutely silent. She would *not* discuss her loss with a man who probably had the sensitivity of the freezing arctic winds that circled the base like hungry predators.

"So what does the lack of a 'second male' have to do with your scientific research here?"

She stared resolutely at a dark spot on the wall past his right shoulder. "My mate was killed by suspected enemies of our planet shortly after we arrived here."

"It was a political murder?" His voice sharpened.

"It's all on file, sir." *Which, he should've read regardless of his so-called duties...*

"Do you think you are in danger?"

"Possibly, but that isn't the main problem. I'm coming to the end of a three year cycle, and my Second Male is dead." She cleared her throat. "I have certain… biological needs that were triggered by finding a mate."

"What kind of needs?"

"Sexual ones."

He leaned back in his chair and regarded her steadily. "What exactly does that entail? Do you go into a breeding cycle like the Kelevans?"

Neeve relaxed slightly. For the first time since he'd taken over the base, she was grateful for his cool, detached manner.

"If I had mates, it would certainly be the time to consider breeding. But in this instance, as I'm alone, it simply means my responses are heightened, and that I would be seeking out my sexual partners."

"Do you become a sexual predator?"

"Nothing quite so dramatic, sir. Everyone on the base is quite safe because none of you are Pavlovan. For three days in each Earth month for the next three months, I will need to be off duty and possibly sedated to control those natural impulses."

"And what if there's an emergency during the time you require off?"

She finally met his gaze and noticed that his eyes were a very dark blue that looked almost as black as his uniform. He was a hard male to fathom, this new commander of theirs. As a telepath she usually found human minds easy to read, but not this man's. He'd developed shields a Pavlovan would be proud of. She had no idea why.

"If I was sedated and the base was under attack, I would have to trust you to make a decision about whether to leave me behind or try and wake me up, sir. I understand that I might be a liability."

He regarded her steadily for a long moment and then

nodded. "I appreciate you telling me this, Doctor. When do you anticipate needing the time off?"

"In the next week or so, sir."

"Then we'll work around you. I've been told to accommodate the needs of our Pavlovan guests very carefully indeed."

Neeve raised her chin. "I've never asked for special treatment before, Captain McNeill."

"I wasn't suggesting that you had." He rose to his feet signaling the audience was at an end. He was tall for a human, topping her by a head. "Thank you."

She saluted and walked out, slowly shutting the door behind her, and made her way back to the lab. *Heeze*, that had been embarrassing, but it would've been worse if she suddenly started losing focus during a mission and tried to screw someone. For the captain's benefit, she'd tried to minimize the effect the three days would have on her as she yearned for a mate who was no longer alive. It would be extremely difficult and emotionally devastating. She missed Malke like an amputated limb, but a human male like Captain McNeill, whose species was only just starting to develop telepathic links, wouldn't understand that.

Which was why she'd kept the information to the more practical and physical aspects of her needs. What was strange, and was something she'd decided to keep to herself was that after two years her urge to mate had suddenly returned with a vengeance. With almost no available partners on Earth, she'd assumed her instincts would remain dormant until she returned to Pavlovan and sought out the Oracle to find her another mate. But perhaps she had just been in mourning?

She wished she had someone to ask, but all her family were still on Pavlovan. It was ironic that she'd spent half her life wanting to get away from her home planet and now missed it more than she would ever have believed. Losing Malke had only made things worse, but she'd been determined to finish out her three-year stint and then go back. She had some pride...

She reached her lab and collapsed into her chair. At least that was over. Now all she had to do was focus on her work until the heat took her, and she could sleep the worst of her natural instincts away.

Captain Ian McNeill put down the file he'd been reading and rubbed his eyes. With the lack of natural light within the base, it was difficult to tell what time it was, but he sensed it was late. Dr. Neeve was a very interesting female with abilities Earth scientists were just starting to observe and recognize in the ever-evolving human population. It was a shame her mate had been killed. Despite her desire to keep things away from the personal, he'd sensed her deep grief for her male. She'd reminded him of how he'd felt about losing Leah...

He pushed the darkness away and concentrated on the present. For some reason, the government was on high alert about the latest feud between the Pavlovans and the Etruscans. All base commanders had been ordered to keep a close eye on their off-world personnel.

Not that he *had* many personnel. He could only surmise that he'd finally pissed off someone high enough in rank to get him sent on this shit poor assignment at the end of the frigging world. His particular skill set was hardly useful in a research center, and he certainly hadn't endeared himself to the scientists. But was there more to it than that? Dr. Neeve had mentioned her mate was murdered. Did the government think she needed special protection? Was that why he was there? If so, he wasn't sure if he appreciated becoming someone's bodyguard without being informed about it.

He opened a link to the central military operations room in London, and the disgruntled face of one of his only friends left in the military flashed up.

"What the hell, Mac? It's three o'clock in the morning."

"You're awake and at work, so what's the problem?"

"I was napping."

"Good to know that the security of our planet is in such safe hands."

"Sod off. What do you want?"

"Can you switch to privacy mode?"

"Sure." Dan's face wavered and then reappeared against a blue screen. "This better? Now what's up?"

"Do you know why they assigned me to Nimbus?"

Dan blinked. "Because the commander retired."

"And what else?"

"Oh that." Dan's grin widened. "It's kind of interesting, isn't it?"

"What is?"

"Oh shit, haven't they told you yet? Have you checked your security filters?"

"Just tell me."

"Okay, but promise me you'll check you have them set up right because I'm fairly certain you should have had this information." His smile faded. "You've got one of the Pavlovans up there, right?"

"Yes, a Dr. Neeve."

"You're supposed to be protecting her with your Extra Special Skills."

"I thought we weren't supposed to use them anymore."

"Yeah, well, the experiment is technically over, and the unit disbanded, but they can't change what they did, so they might as well make use of us." Dan scrubbed a hand over his face. "I don't like it any more than you do, but from what I hear you might be the key to her coming out of this latest inter-planetary conflict alive."

"It's that serious?"

"I don't know why this doctor is so important, but they send the best to look after her—you--so you'd better be prepared for anything."

"Fuck." Mac thought about his Pavlovan's impending mating crisis. "This really isn't a good time."

"It never is." Dan's gaze flicked to one side. "I gotta go."

"Thanks for the intel."

Dan's face faded and Mac stared at the blank blue screen.

"Well hell," he murmured. Fingers flying over the keyboard, he called up all seven of the different messaging systems on his tablet and finally located a file in his trash that looked like something his government would send. It took another five minutes to find the necessary security codes to open the fucker, but he managed it at last.

Security priority: Neeve, Doctor of Science. Pavlovan female. A++ class security required and authorized.

Ian read the remainder of the coded message. It was pretty straightforward. He was to guard the Pavlovan with his life from an undisclosed threat. He was cleared to use his augmented powers if necessary.

Now that was unheard of. Mac sat back. Neeve must be a very important person indeed if the military were prepared to use him to protect her. He reread her personal file and that of Malke, the male who had been killed, but there was no more information to be gleaned there. How the hell was he supposed to protect her if she was knocked out for three days? Was he expected to sit by her bed and hold her hand?

Not that it would be a hardship. She was a beautiful woman with pale skin long reddish hair and deep brown eyes. She spoke quietly, but there was an air of authority about her that made others listen. Her scientific research was considered groundbreaking and offered hope to millions of humans with defective gene alignments. Was that why the government really wanted to keep her alive—to benefit their own kind? He wouldn't put it past them.

And she would soon need sex…

Mac shut down the files and detached his mind from his tablet. Whatever the situation, he had the ability to keep her safe. After all, that was what he'd been trained for, not to run a research station in the freezing cold asscrack of the universe.

End of Sample
To continue reading, be sure to pick up The Power of Persuasion at your favorite retailer.

ALSO BY KATE PEARCE

FOR A FULL LIST PLEASE GO TO KATEPEARCE.COM/BOOKS

The Diable Delamere Series
Historical Romance

Regency dukes, disinherited aristocrats and a plot to assassinate the Prince Regent create plenty of problems for all the heroes and heroines as they struggle to trust each other in an ever-changing game of love, deceit and treachery.

.

The Millcastle Series
Historical Romance

On the cusp of the industrial revolution in the northern town of Millcastle the old and the new clash both in matters of business and of the heart. Can love flourish among the rush to make a profit?

.

House of Pleasure / Simply Series
Historical Erotic Romance

Enter a Regency house of pleasure where nothing is forbidden and every sexual desire you have ever imagined can come true...

.

The Sinners Club

Historical Erotic Romance

When intrigue collides with heated passion behind the closed doors of
the Sinners Club there is nowhere left to hide.

.

The Morgan Ranch Series

Contemporary Western Romance

A Northern Californian ranching family torn apart by tragedy
reluctantly return home to discover not everything was as they thought
it was, and that love, and forgiveness can sometimes go hand in hand.

.

The Millers of Morgan Valley Series

Contemporary Western Romance

When the mother you haven't seen for twenty years asks to visit your
family ranch and set the record straight, how will her ex and six adult
children react? The loves and sometimes messy lives of a ranching
family.

.

The Turner Brothers

Contemporary Erotic Western Romance

Three half-brothers find their own uniquely passionate ways to find
the loves of their lives and accept exactly who they are—no holds
barred.

.

The Obsidian Series

Sci-Fi Romance

Join a renegade band of telepaths roaming the galaxy to protect and rescue their race from the evil empire intent on destroying them.

.

Planet Valhalla Series

Sci-Fi/Futuristic Erotic Romance

One human female crash lands on a planet full of men descended from the Vikings, one of whom is the King who claims her as his mate— what could possibly go wrong? A sexy romp through the stars with excessive sex, a touch of humor and some very satisfied women…

.

The Triad Series

Sci-Fi/Futuristic Erotic Romance

Welcome to an imaginary world where civilizations, clash against the new and unknown, where telepaths are revered and reviled, and where your destiny can be preordained by a living oracle. Add in a group of super-soldier telepaths rescued from Earth and forming sexual triads for life becomes even more complex and life changing.

.

The Tribute Series

Sci-Fi/Futuristic *Dark* Erotic Romance

To save their planet from extinction the government will demand everything from the condemned few—willingly or not.

"Fans of no-holds-barred erotic portrayals of non- and quasi-consensual encounters will devour this steamy triptych."

– Publishers Weekly

·

Soul Justice Series

Paranormal Romance

Come and join a San Francisco based secret government department who investigate the monsters under the bed while risking their psychic abilities and even their own lives.

·

The Tudor Vampire Chronicles

Paranormal Historical Romance

Druids, Vampires and the court of King Henry VIII and his many wives form the backbone of this intriguing series as good fights evil through the first ever female Vampire slayer of her line, Rosalind Llewellyn.

·

Kurland St. Mary Mysteries

Historical Mystery

Writing as Catherine Lloyd

Join wounded cavalry hero Major Sir Robert Kurland and Lucy Harrington the rector's eldest daughter as they solve crimes in their quiet little village and gradually learn to appreciate each other.

ABOUT KATE PEARCE

New York Times and *USA Today* bestselling author Kate Pearce was born in England in the middle of a large family of girls and quickly found that her imagination was far more interesting than real life. After acquiring a degree in history and barely escaping from the British Civil Service alive, she moved to California and then to Hawaii with her kids and her husband and set about reinventing herself as a romance writer.

She is known for both her unconventional heroes and her joy at subverting romance clichés. In her spare time she self publishes science fiction erotic romance, historical romance, and whatever else she can imagine. You can find Kate at katepearce.com.

amazon.com/author/katepearce
goodreads.com/katepearce
bookbub.com/authors/kate-pearce
facebook.com/KatePearceAuthor
twitter.com/kate4queen